D1049769

SNATCH CROP

SNATCH CROP

Gerald Hammond

St. Martin's Press
New York

Library of Congress Cataloging-in-Publication Data
Hammond, Gerald
    Snatch crop / Gerald Hammond.
        p.   cm.
    ISBN 0-312-08891-4
    I. Title.
    PR6058.A55456S57   1993
    823'.914—dc20   92-37737
                                                                     CIP

First published in Great Britain by Macmillan London Limited.

First U.S. Edition: February 1993
10 9 8 7 6 5 4 3 2 1

SNATCH CROP

One

When Sir Peter Hay, who is godfather to me as he is to half my friends, practically invites himself to one of Mum's little dinners, I am both pleased and wary. I like the old boy, or even love him in the purest and most platonic sense of the word. He's good company and he has the proverbial heart of gold. But he does head-hunt rather a lot and when the tasks to be carried out are out of the ordinary he has been known to cast an eye in my direction.

At first, I thought that I was off the hook. Mum, presiding in her usual placid and competent way over the table, had also invited a Mrs Thrower and her daughter, who had just moved into a rented house nearby but were comparative newcomers to the district. Mrs Thrower was new to me, a tall and rather regal woman with black hair and perfect skin but just a trace of a moustache. The daughter, Delia, I had met once before. She was a childish but quite pretty twelve-year-old, fair-haired but otherwise a younger miniature of her mother. She had tried to attach herself to me but when, with the best of intentions, I had offered to take her shooting or rabbiting with Uncle Ronnie's ferrets, she had looked at me as though I were the ferret and she a baby bunny and she had gone away and developed a crush on somebody else instead, to my relief.

Sir Peter was devoting himself to Mrs Thrower. Dad, on my other side, was talking to me about the Scottish FITASC Championship and I was listening with half my mind while the other half thought I was going to miss Briesland House. Late sunshine was glowing on the glass and silver that Mum and I had polished so lovingly and which was throwing highlights on to the panelling. I had spent my life in that house. But enough of the conversation between Mrs Thrower and Sir Peter filtered through for me to gather that there had been a recent separation in the Thrower family and Sir Peter, who seemed to have some connection with the absent Mr Thrower, was delicately hinting at the possibility of a reconciliation while Mrs Thrower was hinting, with equal delicacy, that he should mind his own damn business. I decided that Sir Peter, who has a finger in every pie for miles around, had appointed himself peacemaker and that Mum, as well as being his accomplice, was at her self-appointed duty of making the newcomers feel at home.

Mum was left with the task of entertaining Delia and she was making heavy weather of it. The girl seemed to have little interest in anything but the boys at her school and the latest trend in teenage fashions, neither being a subject in which Mum had more than a polite interest.

I decided to help out. 'What a pretty bracelet,' I said. And so it was. It was a cheap thing of tiny glass beads, but in unusual shades of a lavender colour.

My words were the signal for a change of topics and partners. Delia looked down at the bauble. 'Daddy gave it to me,' she said softly.

'Brought it back to her from Turkey or somewhere,' her mother explained. I noticed that bitter lines were etched

8

around her mouth. 'Quite unsuitable, of course, but it's more than I ever got from him in the way of jewelry.'

Mother, who was wearing a rather good diamond bracelet, tried to hide it under the table and then got up to serve the sweet.

Sir Peter, abandoning his role of mediator, spoke across the table to Dad. 'I've been trying to make sense of my shoot finances,' he said. 'It looks as if I'll have to let three days next season to pay for next year's birds.'

'Don't look at me,' Dad said. 'I can't afford to pay commercial prices for a day's shooting and come away with a brace of birds that have cost me about a hundred quid each. That's expensive poultry.'

Either of them could well have afforded almost unlimited shooting. Sir Peter was the biggest landowner for miles around and Dad was doing very nicely thank you from the gunshop and from his speciality of dealing in antique firearms. But I knew what they meant. Sir Peter ploughed back his considerable income into the land he owned and would have found something immoral in devoting it to his own pleasure, while Dad, like a typical Scot, without being miserly hated to pour money down the drain. He would rather buy a diamond for Mum or a new trap-gun for me than invest in what would soon be no more than a pleasant memory.

'If I looked at you,' Sir Peter said, 'it wasn't as a potential client but as a fellow sufferer.'

Dad nodded sadly. He and Uncle Ronnie run a small family shoot. 'The game dealer's price for pheasants is just ridiculous,' he said.

Again, I knew what they meant. Being Dad's daughter, and Dad being Dad, I had been taken beating not long

9

after I could toddle and had been taught to shoot as soon as I could be trusted to handle a 28-bore safely. In recent years, the Continental market was glutted with pheasants and the British housewife still considered game-birds to be luxury food, forgetting that they were free-range and unadulterated. For this, the trade was largely to blame. The game dealer paid a price for shot pheasants which was a small fraction of what the birds had cost to rear and release, but this saving had never been passed on to the customer. By the time the birds turned up in the poulterer's window, still in the feather, the real value had been more than restored. The loss to the shoots had to be made up from the pockets of the shoot owners, syndicate members or visitors, and it seemed to me that, if those men ever decided that they were fed up with being had for suckers, the loss to both the Scottish economy and ecology would be serious.

'I have been thinking,' Sir Peter said. Dad and I looked at him and even Mum's flow of conversation checked for a moment. Those words usually meant that a conclusion had been reached and something drastic was about to happen.

'Go on,' Dad said.

'Two adjacent units are vacant in the industrial estate. Choice Chicks went bust during the salmonella scare and the meat pie factory's closing. BSE in beef,' Sir Peter added in unnecessary explanation. He looked down at his sweet for the first time. 'Ah. Apple tart! Nobody ever caught anything from an apple. Shame that you can't say as much for a tart.' He paused and harumphed at his own joke. Mrs Thrower looked shocked. Delia just looked blank.

'Both units are still equipped. So here's an opportunity.

What we need is a co-op of the major shoots. And the minor ones, for the matter of that. Cut out the middleman and start a company to popularise the pheasant. Oven-ready, free-range birds at affordable prices. We even have a ready-made outlet. The fish-vans are being hit by the cuts in North Sea quotas.'

There was silence for a few seconds. Mrs Thrower was still rattling on about the difficulties of bringing up a daughter without a man in the house, but that was no more than a sort of verbal Muzak and hardly counted.

'What about capital?' Dad said at last.

'Not a great deal required if the factories are rented. The shoots would put up what was needed. Others would soon want to join in when they saw that they could get a better return on their bag, and late-comers could pay a premium to pay off the first investors. Two commercial organisers and four private estates are already keen. How about you?'

Dad had already made up his mind. 'I'll have to speak to Ronnie and Wal,' he said. (Wallace was his partner in the business and a member of the shoot.) 'If the figures look good, we're in.'

The subject seemed to be exhausted. I turned my attention to the other half of the table but Delia, despite her mother's best efforts, was now monopolising the conversation. She was rattling on about some birthday party, to the acute boredom of her listeners.

Sir Peter, however, was still riding his new hobby-horse. 'Some of the staff are willing to stay on or come back,' he said. 'But, of course, we'll need an overall manager. I thought that you, Deborah, might take it on.'

Caught with my guard down, I nearly said that I was

too busy. That excuse would have been demolished with contumely. For years, Dad and Sir Peter had been in the habit of tossing me in off the deep end whenever there was some tedious management chore to be undertaken, but for the moment I had made a comfortable little nest for myself in the local scene. I trained as a engraver but I can do most jobs around the gunsmith's bench and had been helping Dad out whenever that side of the business, or any other, called for another pair of hands. My other so-called job, at the Pentland Gun Club, had largely been taken over by the new Secretary and I was only conducting a few coaching sessions a week and organising competitions along lines which had, by now, become so set that any change provoked complaints by the dozen.

'But I'm getting married in August,' I said weakly. 'That's next month,' I added, realising for the first time that events were rushing at me.

'Plenty of time,' Sir Peter said. 'We won't get going until late October. Any wild birds of respectable size will probably be shared among the guests and what pheasants you're offered before November will either be immature or badly shot up. Or they'll be birds frozen and held over from last season.'

'But why me? I don't know anything about the poultry trade.'

'You know all the keepers,' he pointed out. 'You, if anybody, can get them to deliver good birds that aren't turning green or covered in flies' eggs. We'll have plenty of competent work-staff. What we need is somebody to pull it together and make it work. I've seen you in action before now. You can organise.'

'And you love bossing people around,' Dad said. He

12

sounded amused. Evidently he was not going to help me out by pleading that my services could not be spared.

'Not the keepers,' I said. 'They're more used to shouting at me to keep in line.'

'You do yourself less than justice,' said Sir Peter. 'You're good at getting people to jump through hoops.'

'Only men,' Mum said. She had been taking it all in despite Delia's prattle. She was laughing at me too.

'What's more,' Dad said, 'you'll need a proper salary when you and Ian set up house.'

'It'll be very seasonal,' I objected.

'If it is,' Dad said, 'you'll be able to keep up your competition shooting. You can't expect Ian's salary to stretch that far.'

'It may not be so seasonal,' Mum said. 'Is there a good cold store?'

'Yes indeed,' said Sir Peter.

'You'll get a proportion of birds which have been shot from too close or chewed by a beater's dog. Boil them down into pheasant gravy, buy up pigeon and rabbits outside the game season and make game pies.'

'They'd have us under the Trades Description Act,' I said. 'Pigeon and rabbit aren't game.'

'I think we'd be all right if the contents were printed on the bag,' Sir Peter said thoughtfully. 'I'll find out.'

Nobody bothered to ask me whether I was going to take it on. The matter seemed to be settled.

'Pigeon and rabbit pie with pheasant gravy,' Mrs Thrower said thoughtfully. 'It doesn't sound very tasty.'

Sir Peter smiled at her, almost laughing. 'What did you think Mrs Calder gave us for the main course?' he asked her.

'That? But it was delicious!' Mrs Thrower said. Her tone suggested that Sir Peter had to be mistaken if not lying.

'I'm glad you enjoyed it,' Mum said. 'I'll give you the recipe if you like. Coffee, anybody?'

I tried to explain that I didn't want a job, I just wanted to be a good wife and, in the fullness of time, a mother, but nobody seemed to be listening.

My wedding day arrived in a rush and found us more or less prepared. It was as much of an endurance test as I had expected.

Ian and I had been 'going steady', as they say, for several years. We enjoyed each other's company, shared fits of helpless laughter at the same trivia and felt a strong physical attraction. If that is love, then we loved. Marriage seemed an inevitable goal.

Ian Fellowes had been a detective sergeant with Lothian and Borders, stationed in Newton Lauder but responsible to Edinburgh. When, at long last and after considerable campaigning and politicking by the local Superintendent, it was decided to upgrade Criminal Investigation in the area and Ian went up to Inspector, with a detective sergeant of his own and two constables thrown in as makeweights, there seemed to be no reason to wait any longer. He was now settled and almost adequately paid.

We would have been quite happy with a civil ceremony. Marriage, after all, is no more than a contract to stay together and be faithful, which is exactly what we intended to do. Mum had conscientiously dragged me to kirk and Sunday school during my childhood and for a few years I had felt the eye of God following me around so unblinkingly that I had taken to undressing in the dark. And then, one day, I had suddenly said to myself, 'But this doesn't make sense,' and that was an end to it. So the idea of being gift-wrapped and 'given away' to my chosen man seemed impossibly archaic and sexist.

But Mum had made up her mind that her only baby was going to have the church wedding, which, for some reason that I never got to the bottom of, she had never had for herself. Dad had been paying into an endowment fund for more than twenty years and he topped it up by selling one of his favourite muzzle-loaders, a flintlock – by Manton no less! We went through with it and suffered all the ritual embarrassment. I was not even strong-minded enough to refuse the services of the insipid Delia as bridesmaid. 'Poor child,' Mum said, 'she doesn't have a proper father any more,' and that was that. Dad, looking like the more handsome sort of elder statesman in his hired morning suit, gave me away while Delia, with her fair prettiness, looked as if she had been sculpted out of ice-cream.

The church was packed. Dad, who gets expansive when he has taken a social dram, had been issuing invitations broadcast and as I went up the aisle on his arm I thought that I recognised the backs of several quite unexpected necks. Returning, this time with Ian, I could see the faces and decided that Dad must have invited everybody who looked even vaguely familiar.

Ian's colleagues – including, astonishingly, Superintendent Munro – formed a guard of honour. At the hotel, we managed to smile through most of the speeches. Sir Peter, looking almost smart in his best kilt, made by far the best speech, lasting less than a minute, and, as they say, brought the house down. My Uncle Ronnie, who was not scheduled to speak but who had been mixing champagne and whisky with the occasional, accidental sherry, then got to his feet and spoke at some length in a dialect so thick that few of those present could follow him. For this I was thankful as most of his speech was composed of scurrilous anecdotes from my past. How my well-spoken mum came to have a brother with the appearance and the social grace of a demented gorilla still amazes me.

We would have sneaked away as soon as the meal was finished, leaving the company to enjoy our wedding in their own ways. Unfortunately it had leaked out that we were spending the first night within a taxi-ride (the exact destination being a well-guarded secret) and any attempt at escape was sternly resisted. Ian, who is a rotten dancer but almost good-looking in his morning suit, led me out and soon most of the company was on the floor. Dad, I noticed, was dancing carefully with young Delia, who was better at it than he was, while her mother had been dragged, protesting, on to the floor by Uncle Ronnie and was, as usual, exuding an aura of Suffering Bravely.

Several duty dances later, I was hoping at least to get back to the top table and kick off the bridal slippers, but a guest claimed me. This was one of the surprise attenders – Sir Humphrey Peace, the owner of a medium-sized estate to the south of the town. I had in the past gone beating for him, shot with him and even, with Dad and Mum, dined at his house, so that I knew him without ever having got to know him, if you can make sense of that. In a lean and rather delicate way he looked and acted very much as part of the Establishment. I would have put his reserve down to his being one of the many older men who are shy of younger women, except that the men of my family seemed similarly to be kept at arm's length. Snobbery is so rare in the Borders that it never occurred to me that he might just feel that we were beneath his notice. His presence at my wedding (preceded by a set of crystal sherry glasses) could only be explained by the fact that Dad is a useful person for the shooting man to keep in with.

Sir Humphrey steered me several times around the floor without saying a word. When the band came to a halt, he spoke for the first time. 'Wish you every happiness,' he said abruptly. 'Sadly, I'll have to leave now. Business calls.'

We had come to a halt near the door and, as he turned towards it, another of the surprise guests entered, apologising over his shoulder to Dad for missing both the service and the meal. I had only set eyes on Nigel Farquharson, the laird of Boyes Castle many miles to the north, three or four times before but I recognised him immediately. There was no mistaking the large, big-bellied figure nor the hooked nose and the eyes half hidden by the puffed flesh. The two men almost collided and then looked at each other blankly.

'You do know each other?' I asked.

'No,' Sir Humphrey said. 'Should we?'

I performed a quick introduction. They shook hands guardedly.

There was an awkward pause.

'I think,' Mr Farquharson said loftily, 'that you once shot a friend of mine.'

This was about as complete a put-down as I have ever heard, but Sir Humphrey looked genuinely amused. 'Then he must have moved away from his peg,' he said. He sounded, for him, quite genial.

The two men nodded and moved apart.

I changed out of my wedding dress and we ran the

gauntlet and escaped as soon as we decently could. The whole affair was one of those occasions, like a visit to the dentist, which are hell at the time but when they're over you're glad you did it.

We flew to Cyprus, taking our shotguns with us. There was a major clay pigeon tournament on and we both entered; but our minds were on other things and our reflexes were slow. I think that my reaction time had gone out to about ten seconds. It was the first time in years that I hadn't even taken the ladies' bronze, but I didn't care. And that is all that I intend to say about our honeymoon.

We came back to Ian's small flat in Newton Lauder instead of to the dated Victorian charm of Briesland House two miles outside the town. I was now Mrs Fellowes instead of Miss Calder. And Ian and I could now share a bed.

Everything was different and yet life was much the same. We were hardly back when Dad gave me, as an extra wedding present, Sam, the semi-retired Labrador who had been my companion all through my teens. Sam had been more my dog than Dad's anyway, as I pointed out to him. 'But what,' I asked, 'am I supposed to do with Sam while I'm away slaving over the hot stove that you and Sir Peter have lumbered me with?'

'We can keep him for you at the shop,' Dad said. 'You'll be passing the door, morning and evening.' Which was all very well for Dad, who avoided serving in the shop as much as he could. Wallace might not be pleased to have a pair of hungry eyes following him around.

I took Sam along for a day at the grouse at Sir Peter's invitation, although Sir Peter himself was busy elsewhere.

Ian and Sam and I had a big day decoying pigeons and when September came in we wasted a couple of very early mornings in going to the foreshore in search of the first duck of the season.

Ian had raised no objection to my being a working wife and, after my initial resistance had waned, I began to work up enthusiasm for the project. Sir Peter, it seemed, was very busy with some ploy of his own and little had been done except to sign the lease for the two small units. But, to my dismay, he had taken one step that I would rather he had left to me. He had engaged a secretary. This was Mrs Thrower. She needed the job now that her husband was no longer bringing home an income, she explained – as though working was somehow more of a disgrace than being deserted for a younger woman – and the sale of the family home had brought in little more than enough to pay off the mortgage. She seemed competent enough, but she was eternally sorry for herself and although she seemed reluctant to take the smallest decision on my behalf she let me see that in her view I was far too young to be her boss.

It was left to me to prepare for business and I began to work flat out. The machinery had to be overhauled, small equipment and materials purchased. Mum was a heaven-sent source of sound advice.

If I waited too long, the redundant workers would all have found jobs elsewhere, yet I was not going to take them on and pay them to stand idle. In desperation, I went out at night with Uncle Ronnie, lamping for rabbits with a .22 rifle from his Land Rover and for three nights in a row we filled the back of his vehicle. The local pigeon-shooters were doing good business over the rape and barley stubbles

19

and game dealers' prices had fallen through the floor. I bought the lot and some frozen pheasants left over from the previous January. A neighbouring business printed up freezer-bags for me.

My newly hired staff were kept hard at it, skinning and plucking, cleaning, cooking, bagging-up and freezing. For a day or two I was near panic, wondering whether I hadn't overreached myself. Money was dribbling away and I might be on the brink of a financial disaster. But I spent some time flirting with a reporter on the local rag and he gave us several column inches on the subject of free-range, organic meat. Then I struck a deal with a supermarket manager. In exchange for a cut-throat bulk price for bacon and Irish mushrooms, I presented him with our first gross and a half of bagged and frozen pie-fillers. He made them his loss-leader for a few days and they caught on. The fish-vans, as Sir Peter had predicted, were desperate for other lines and they began to push our wares.

But it was for the pheasants and other game-birds that the business had been set up. It had been a dry summer and by late October good pheasants were coming on the market and the price was already slumping. We were paying slightly above the going rate. Other shoots beside the original members were bringing us their birds. The game dealer, who was doing well with venison, was, if anything, rather relieved. Three more estates applied for membership. More outlets had opened up and, thanks in part to some inexpensive advertising, the oven-ready birds moved well. I began to have some time to spare for housewifely duties and Ian seemed pleased to escape from a diet of game pies.

If business was developing well, I was saved from complacency by a series of minor irritations. Mrs Thrower's air of superiority was a constant annoyance. Her frequent grumbles about the accountant husband who had deserted her depressed me. He had, it seemed, vanished completely and might have been dead except for the occasional money order – totally inadequate, according to Mrs Thrower – which arrived through the post at irregular intervals. When I tried to imagine how I would feel if Ian treated me the same way I was inclined to be sympathetic, but that only encouraged more bouts of self-pity and made me feel that in Mr Thrower's shoes I would have taken similar evasive action.

Because the school was only a street or two away, Delia came straight to us for the last couple of hours of the working day. Any objection on my part only provoked a monologue from Mrs Thrower on the subject of the dangers awaiting a young girl in the streets, although Newton Lauder was not noted for rapine and I thought that Delia's preoccupation with boys who had barely attained puberty (and had no idea what to do with it) made her relatively proof against seduction. We tried to get her to earn some pocket-money by fetching and carrying or vacuuming up the downy feathers which permeated the place, but she preferred to make a nuisance of herself, pestering the girls for attention and interfering with the machinery. I was tempted to stuff her into the plucking machine or one of the boiling pans but nobly resisted the temptation.

One evening, when the play we were watching had finished, Ian used the remote control to kill the television. Sam, who had been snoozing on the hearth-rug, took it as a signal that his evening walk was due and began to struggle to his feet. 'Apart from Mrs Thrower's word for it,' Ian said, 'have you seen or heard anything to convince you that she doesn't know where her husband is?'

Sam recognised the signs and lay down again.

I thought it over. The question seemed to be carefully worded to obscure the reasoning behind it. Ian was very meticulous about not betraying police secrets at home, which usually suited me. There are more interesting topics for pillow talk. But this was of direct concern to me. 'What exactly do you want to know?' I asked him.

'Let's just pretend that I'm a police officer and that you're a member of the public who happens to be her employer. Well?'

'Very well, officer,' I said. 'No, there haven't been any visits or phone calls, and if there have been any letters they didn't come to the factory and she hasn't shown them to me.'

'That's what I thought,' he said. He changed the subject quickly and a few minutes later he went out with Sam.

Next day, watching Mrs Thrower typing up invoices, the question and answer came back to me. It seemed that Ian suspected that the Throwers were still in touch, which suggested some sort of conspiracy. It was an hour later before a more obvious explanation struck me. Ian suspected that Mrs Thrower had murdered her husband. Perhaps they were even now digging up the garden of the house where they had once lived together.

The idea, incredible at first, soon took on a macabre credibility. Mrs Thrower was not a very clever woman but she had a strong and ruthless personality. That, coupled with her obvious bitterness, made her, in my mind, a potential murderess. Soon, I found that I was passing our few conversations through a mental filter in search of any implication that I might be a danger to her.

This was getting to be a bit of a pain in something or other. When Mrs Thrower was next in a talkative state I tried to turn her grumbling into disgorging of information.

I decided on an oblique approach. 'Were there no warning signs?' I asked her. 'Or did he just vanish?'

She gave what I can only describe as a bitter laugh. 'There were all the usual signs,' she said. 'Saying that he was kept late at the office but not answering on his private line. Traces of perfume that I wouldn't wear for a bet.' She looked at me as if wondering whether I were too young for such confidences and then seemed to decide that, as a young married woman, I had probably found out about the horrors of sex by now. 'That I didn't mind as long as he was discreet about it – we had put that sort of thing behind us. If sex was so important to him, let him get on with it. I thought he'd get it out of his system. I certainly never expected him to pack a few bags while I was out of the house.' The harsh lines around her mouth deepened. 'Left me a note, if you please, to say that he'd gone off with somebody else and wouldn't be coming back. And then he had the impertinence to ask me in a PS to give Delia his love.'

'He's probably fed up with the other woman by now. Have you asked him to come back?'

'Writing through his solicitors? That's the only address I have for him. I have more pride than that. Anyway, I wouldn't have him back now. The damage is done.' She sniffed, haughtily rather than tearfully, and went back to her typing.

She was so obviously suffering from hurt pride rather than a broken heart that I knew she had to be telling the truth. All in all, I decided, the Throwers were the millstones round my neck.

I was soon to be relieved of one of them.

In early November, Sir Peter arrived suddenly with Wallace James, Dad's partner, and they spent the afternoon going over the figures. Wal began his working life as an accountant and Sir Peter often begged his help in interpreting figures. Wallace pronounced himself satisfied and left to relieve Dad at the shop. Sir Peter settled down in the office. He congratulated Mrs Thrower on her books and she half-bowed in her queenly way, which was a piece of impertinence – I had pulled her up more than once for sloppy book-keeping and had ended up doing most of the work myself.

He turned his attention to me. 'As for you, my dear,' he said, 'you've done wonders already. If you go on like this, the subscribing shoots can expect a good dividend at the end of the season and there'll be a bonus for yourself. For both of you, in fact.'

I made modest and grateful noises but Mrs Thrower just bowed again.

'And now,' Sir Peter said, 'I'd like a word in private with Mrs Thrower on quite another matter. May we use this office?'

This was a polite way of inviting me to go for a walk. I could hardly refuse. Mrs Thrower seemed neither surprised nor apprehensive, so I left them to it and went out to supervise the cleaning-up and scrubbing-out that marked the end of the day. Whenever I caught sight of them through the glass of the office partition I thought that Mrs Thrower was being her usual querulous self but that Sir Peter looked more anxious than he usually allowed the world to see. He was looking old. That gave me a sudden feeling of unease. All my life, he had looked the same – a rather scarecrow figure with a bush of untidy grey hair, dressed in one or another of his shabby kilts. The revelation that he might after all be mortal kicked away one of my foundation-stones.

Just as the work was finishing, Ian turned up to take me home. I looked at him, to be sure that he had not also aged suddenly, but he was the same man, young for his new rank, square-faced, red-haired, snub-nosed and built to last for ever. I felt secure again.

When the staff had gone and we were ready to leave, Sir Peter and Mrs Thrower came out of the office. She looked around her. 'Where's Delia?' she asked me.

'I haven't seen her,' I said. 'I thought you must have arranged to collect her from a friend's house.'

We all looked pale under the fluorescent lights of the factory unit, but Mrs Thrower had lost what little colour had been left to her. 'Definitely not,' she said. 'She was supposed to come straight here.' She ran to the door and threw it open. 'Delia!'

There was no answer. She turned uncertainly to face us. 'Damn, damn, damn!' she said.

'Keep calm,' Sir Peter said. 'She'll probably turn up at any moment. Probably been kept late at school.'

Mrs Thrower looked at her watch and shook her head.

I looked around for Ian. He had gone into the office. I saw him put down the phone. He came out. 'There's been no report of an accident,' he said. 'No incidents at all. The uniformed branch will keep an eye out for her. What do you want to do?'

'You should wait here for a while,' Sir Peter said to Mrs Thrower, 'in case she shows up or telephones. You could phone the school and the homes of any of her friends. And your own house, of course, in case she's misunderstood you and gone straight home. I'll go and look around for her.'

'That would be best,' Ian said. 'It's too early to involve us – the police – officially. If there's nothing I can do for the moment I'll go and eat and then phone you at home.'

It seemed callous to walk away. 'Would you like me to stay with you?' I asked her.

She shook her head again. Her expression suggested that I was a contemporary of Delia and would probably be more trouble than I was worth.

'We'll go then,' I said. From the door, I looked back. 'Don't worry. She's probably in some friend's house, watching television.'

'I don't allow her to watch television.'

'Never?'

'Never.'

My face must have shown my surprise and disapproval. Any form of unnecessary censorship strikes me as silly and probably counter-productive. It makes the subject more interesting and introduces the great difficulty of drawing lines between undefinable areas – or, like Mrs Thrower, leaping to the illogical extreme. Ignorance in a young girl is not protection. 'There is nothing on it but sex,' she added defensively. 'Sex, sex, sex, sex, sex.'

'Listen,' I said to Ian. 'She's singing our song.' I spoke softly but she probably heard me.

Two

Ian, as usual, drove the car through the dark streets. To celebrate his new rank and his new status as a married man he had taken advantage of a nought-per-cent finance offer and traded in his old banger for a brand-new hatchback. Neither of us could be sure that our marriage would have survived if I had put a scratch on its mint paintwork.

We collected Sam and installed him in the back. 'Delia's probably only playing her mother up,' I said. 'All the same, let's zig and zag a bit, going home.'

We zigged and zagged, twice passing Sir Peter. There was no sign of Delia. We stopped to speak to the only group of children on streets which had been emptied by mealtime, but none of them had seen her since school.

'We'd better go and eat,' Ian said at last.

'It's not like you to come away when a child's gone missing.'

'If she's still missing in an hour's time, I'll start the ball rolling,' he said. 'After that, I may not have time to eat.'

I let it go for the moment. 'Sir Peter's looking his age all of a sudden,' I said.

Ian brought the car to rest, very gently, outside the flat. 'I think he'll pass his next MOT,' he said lightly. 'And the one after that.'

The night was wet. He held an umbrella over me as though I would dissolve between the car and the front door. I headed for the kitchenette and began to scramble a quick meal together and another for Sam. With both of us working, we only managed what Mum would have considered to be 'proper' meals at weekends. We usually took a mild drink, to mark the change from work to leisure, but although he brought me my usual weak gin and tonic I noticed that he forewent his dram of whisky.

We sat down to a sort of mixed grill with microwaved vegetables, followed by fruit, biscuits and cheese and coffee. Even Mum could not have done better in the time.

'Now,' I said, 'what are you holding back?'

'How do you mean?'

'Don't be evasive,' I said sternly. 'If you start answering a question with a question I'll start withholding your marital privileges. Young Delia's gone missing. She may have been kidnapped or even murdered. If any other young girl in the town failed to show up after school, you'd be dashing around like a chicken with its head cut off. And not long ago, you suspected Mrs Thrower of having murdered her husband. For all I know, you still do. And yet you accept Delia's disappearance without a quiver. So there's something I don't know.'

'There's a lot you don't know,' he said gently. 'For a start, when did I ever say that we suspected her of disposing of her husband?'

'When did you ever say a damn thing?' I retorted.

'Now who's answering a question with a question?' he said, doing it himself. 'Let me assure you of one thing. It seemed possible that Mr Thrower had been done away

28

with, and it still does seem on the cards. But if that turns out to be so, his widow will figure very low on the list of suspects.'

'If you'd told me that, I needn't have made myself dizzy turning round so as not to let her get behind me.' Another thought came to me. 'Sir Peter was having an earnest and private talk with Mrs T just before you arrived. He's been too busy to come and poke his nose into the running of the business, and that isn't like him. He brought Wallace James with him and Wallace doesn't usually still do accountancy. Dad's been too busy to shoot, so my guess is that Wal's been neglecting the shop because Sir Peter's working his backside off. So what's going on? Don't tell me that there isn't a connection.'

'I don't think I should talk about it,' he said.

'Why not? You've discussed your cases with me in the past.'

He put down his fork and looked at me. 'Those were cases in which you were already involved,' he said. 'Or else they concerned folk you didn't know and weren't likely to meet. This time, you know the people. If they care to tell you all about it, that's their business. But can't you see that it would be wrong for me to tell you their secrets? Please?'

I couldn't; but I could see that it would be wrong for me to add to his worries. 'Of course,' I said. 'Don't worry about it. I'll screw it out of Sir Peter when I see him again.'

I saw him relax. 'You do that,' he said. 'You know, I've been dreading the day when I'd have to break it to you that I can't always discuss things openly. But it didn't hurt very much, did it? I'll tell you this much and no more, and don't you go quoting me. It's possible that something terrible may have happened. But, on the balance of probabilities, I think not. And if what's happened is what I think happened, it may even turn out to be for the best, one way or the other.'

'Let's hope you're right,' I said.

We both breathed more easily. I still felt cheated, but a crisis had gone past.

He finished his meal and went to the phone. He must have called Mrs Thrower at her home. 'I'll have to go out,' he told me. 'I may not be very long.'

'You'll probably be all night,' I said.

'No. If there's no word by morning, that'll be time enough to start the emergency routine.'

He gave me a hug and left. I used the blank evening to dash around the flat – like a chicken with its head cut off, as I had said to Ian – catching up with all the neglected housework and trying to prepare meals for the next day or two.

He came back at ten. 'Nothing to worry about yet,' he said. He refused to tell me any more and I refused to be more than a little bit hurt by his secretiveness. If policemen told their wives everything, I assured myself, there would soon be no secrets left. We went to bed early and I let him see that he was forgiven and that my earlier threat had been an idle one. It did not take him long to get my message.

In the morning, he was on the phone before I had even started to make breakfast. I could have overheard whatever he said, but he said nothing except for his own name. The remainder of his end of the conversation consisted of grunts and a quick goodbye. When he came to the table he was looking thoughtful.

'Nothing?' I asked him.

He shook his head. 'We should hear soon. If we don't, I'll start to get really worried.'

'If you want volunteers for search-parties,' I began.

Again the headshake. 'Too early for that,' he said. 'But I'll set enquiries going.'

To my surprise Mrs Thrower, who was not usually among our more punctual arrivals, was already in the office when I reached the factory. She looked drawn but had herself under control.

'If you'd rather be at home, I'll understand,' I said.

'I'd just as soon keep occupied,' she said.

'All right. But if there's anything I can do . . . ?'

She looked at me with her eyebrows up. 'What on earth could you do?' she asked. Before I had time to take offence she went on. 'Only the lawyers can do anything now.'

'Lawyers?' I said. 'I don't understand.'

'My husband,' she said patiently. 'He's the one who'll have taken her. I'm sure of it.'

She spoke as if I were dim-witted, as she often did. This time, I suppose, she was correct. The lack of a general panic was explained. 'I didn't think of that,' I said weakly. I felt myself relax and only then realised that I had been living through the horrors of abduction, abuse and murder with the absent Delia. Once, when I was a child, I had been carried off as a hostage against Dad's interference in a criminal matter. I had almost forgotten the incident, but it must still have been looming somewhere in my subconscious mind.

'Your husband didn't tell you?'

'Certainly not,' I said indignantly. 'It would be quite wrong for him to discuss confidential matters with me.'

'I suppose that's true,' she said, 'as far as it goes. I was thinking the same thing myself.' She put her head down over the typewriter. If she had not been Sir Peter's choice for the post I would have fired her on the spot, Delia or no Delia. She looked up again after typing a few lines. 'If the bastard thinks he can force me to give him a better deal in the divorce, he can think again.'

'He may just want custody of Delia,' I said.

'He never gave a damn about her. Delia adored him, but that didn't matter to him.' She was going to say more but she bit it off and went back to her typing.

Later in the morning, she went out to do a thousand and one business errands in the town. Gathering up her gloves and handbag, she paused at my desk. 'If there are any messages for me, take a note of them,' she said.

Ten minutes later, while I was still seething at her calm assumption that I was her secretary (instead of vice versa), Sir Peter arrived looking for her.

'She's out,' I told him. 'You could try the bank or the post office. Or you could wait. I'll make coffee.'

'Don't bother with that,' he said absently. But he dropped into the visitor's chair. 'When she comes back, would you tell her that we've sent messages through her husband's solicitors and through the bank that's been transmitting money to her.'

It was unfair to blame Sir Peter for another example of role reversal but my expression must have shown irritation. 'You don't get on with her, do you, my dear?' he said.

'She has the knack of putting my back up,' I admitted.

'I can see how she might.' He studied me solemnly for a moment. 'When I give you the word, you can get rid of her as fast as you like. But for the moment I'd be grateful if you'd put up with her.'

'You can be just as annoying,' I said. 'You read my mind. I wasn't going to fire her while this was hanging over her head. After that . . . '

'After that, she may not be around these parts anyway. Until then, I'd be grateful if you'd just keep an eye on her.'

It was as quiet in the office as it could be with the preparation-room staff working and chattering a few yards away. 'Keep an eye in what sense?' I asked. 'Protective or nosy?'

'The one you do best.'

'Protective?'

He half smiled. 'Nosy.'

'You'd better tell me what the hell is going on,' I said.

He made a small gesture of helpless apology. 'I can't,' he said. 'The whole matter's as confidential as . . . as next year's budget. For the moment, I can only tell you that we're very anxious to get in touch with Mr Thrower – if he's still alive.'

'He must be alive,' I said. 'Or he couldn't have taken Delia. Surely?'

Sir Peter started to say something, checked himself and began again. The plucking machine had started up next door and he had to raise his voice to be heard. 'The police rather favoured the theory that he'd been knocked on the head. I suppose that their minds learn to work that way. Mine follows more fiscally oriented lines. There's been more than a little financial hocus-pocus going on. Mr Thrower may or may not have been involved, but the way he walked out of his job at Sempylene, if it was voluntary, plus the fact that he's still managing to send money to his family, makes it look bad for him. And we can't be sure that Mrs Thrower isn't in it with him. That's all I can say and even that may be too much. We've managed to keep it under wraps so far and it's got to stay that way.'

'I shan't spread it around,' I promised him.

'You never were a chatterbox. Not, at least, since you first entered your teens and had some secrets of your own to keep.'

Without my even thinking about the matter, a nasty suspicion popped into my head. 'This business with Delia,' I said. 'It isn't a put-up job?'

He blinked at me. 'What made you think of that?'

'I don't know,' I said. 'It occurred to me that you wanted him to come out into the open and that this might be the one certain way to make him show himself. Or his solicitors might not be willing to cough up his address over a civil matter, but a kidnapping would be something different. And I just wondered. You tycoons can play rough.'

'This is more likely to drive him deeper underground. All the same, I wish I'd thought of it myself. I'm almost flattered to be thought of as a tycoon and a devious mastermind,' he said. He got up. 'Please give her my message. And if you notice anything out of key, especially if you've any reason to believe that she's in touch with him, give me a ring. Or tell that husband of yours.'

I hesitated. I disliked Mrs Thrower, but not enough to spy on her. On the other hand, if two out of my three favourite men wanted to know what was going on . . .

'All right,' I said.

He nodded gratefully and pottered out, looking vague.

He always looked vague. It was the camouflage behind which he hid a very sharp mind.

Mrs Thrower phoned later from the bank. She had asked for a statement and their version of the balance did not agree with ours. I read her some figures over the phone. She thought that the bank had credited a cheque to somebody else's account. My guess was that she had entered an incoming cheque twice, but I left her to find out for herself. She was staying to go over the figures with one of the cashiers and I preferred the factory without her.

Mr Thrower, I decided, had to be alive. Otherwise, I thought, why would anyone want to kidnap Delia? There did not seem to be any money for a ransom and personally I wouldn't have had her as a gift (or 'in a lucky bag', as Mum would have said). Unless her father had been deep in the 'financial hocus-pocus' and somebody else wanted to screw it out of his widow. Or unless there was a rapist-murderer on the loose after all.

Madge Foullis, the preparation-room chargehand, claimed my attention before I could think myself into a case of nerves. The weather had been damp but unseasonably warm, there had not been enough overnight frost to knock off the insects and some of my last purchase of pheasants had been badly stored by the estate and were slightly flyblown. I made a note to give the keeper a stern warning and showed Madge how to deal with eggs, but I told her to keep the batch separate and that any sign of maggots was to be referred to me, when the whole lot would be returned and the cheque stopped.

A man had come in and was standing by the office door. From his aggressive stance I took him for a meat inspector and my heart missed a beat. Wallace and Dad were both away and Janet, Wallace's wife, had charge of the shop. She had disliked Sam ever since he had raided her shopping basket about ten years earlier and she refused to have him in the shop with her. So Sam was under my desk and the last time the meat inspector had caught him there he had raised the roof. But this man was too neatly dressed.

'I'm looking for my wife,' he said when I approached him. 'I'm Bernard Thrower.'

'She's out for the moment,' I said. I looked at him with some curiosity. It took me a few seconds to pin down the discrepancy between his looks and his manner. Then it came to me that he moved and spoke as if under a strain, which was hardly surprising. Take away the hunted look and the anger and the cast of his features would have suggested somebody both amicable and calm. Dad operated on the theory that any two people who look alike will probably behave alike, and several men of my acquaintance with the same tall build, long head and wide-set eyes had been placid by temperament.

There was another contradiction. His fair colouring and pale eyelashes suggested that he was the genetic source of Delia's blonde hair, but he had removed his tweed hat in a belated gesture of politeness and his hair was almost too black to be true. It was also growing out fair at the parting, I noticed.

'My lawyers phoned me. They said that Delia's disappeared? Is it true?'

'All I know is that her mother expected her to come here after school yesterday and she didn't turn up,' I said. 'As far as I know, she hasn't turned up yet.'

He glared at me as though it were all my fault. 'What's being done about it?'

36

'I don't know. You needn't take it out on me,' I added. 'I'm the original innocent bystander. I think they were going to start a search if she hadn't been heard of today. The most widely accepted theory seemed to be that you'd got her.'

Some of the anger went out of him, to be replaced by anxiety. 'Tell me honestly. This isn't a trick?'

'Not as far as I know,' I said. 'Bear in mind that I don't have a tenth of the facts. But your wife seemed genuinely horrified when Delia didn't show up here last night. The police seem to be concerned. So does Sir Peter Hay, who seems to be involved somehow. I got the impression that the only reason they weren't all in a state of panic was that they were fairly sure that you'd got her.'

He was studying my face as I spoke. I must have passed some sort of test, because he nodded. 'Thank you,' he said. 'I believe you. Tell them that they can start to panic now. The message to my lawyers suggested that I might have taken her. I wish to God that I had! As soon as it reached me, I set off to come here and tell my wife that I had damn-all to do with it. You can tell her that with my compliments.' He paused and his manner became almost pleading. 'I want to have Delia with me, but not that way. And, if anybody's interested, you can tell them that I dropped out to start a new life with Elaine. Whatever went on at Sempylene, I didn't touch a penny; and I'll sue anybody who says different.'

'Wouldn't it be better to say so yourself?' I asked him. 'Sir Peter Hay's been trying to get in touch with you.'

'Impossible,' he said. 'I can't explain to you, but it's quite impossible. I'm as innocent a bystander as you are, caught up in something I can't control.'

I could feel panic rising in me, on Delia's behalf. 'What do you think has happened to her?' I asked.

'I wish I knew for sure.' His eyes altered focus, looking through me towards some hell beyond. 'Poor kid! Please God they haven't hurt her. I'm only guessing, but I think – I hope – that she may have been taken to put pressure on me. In which case she should be all right . . . if I don't hang around here.'

'Then you'd better get going,' I said. I felt suddenly sorry for him. 'I hope it works out for all of you. If there's anything I can do, this side of lawbreaking . . . '

'Thanks,' he said gruffly. He looked hard into my face again. 'You really mean that, don't you? Yes, there is one thing. If – when – they get Delia back safe, they'll send a message through my solicitors. Then I'll come and talk to the police. That should end the danger to Delia and I can look after myself. But I don't want to be tricked.' He took a pencil and a blank invoice off my desk and wrote down the phone number of his solicitors. 'When you, yourself, see Delia safe and well, phone them. I'll know it's genuine if you say that the message comes from . . . what's your Christian name?'

'Deborah,' I told him.

'You'll do that? And no tricks?'

'I promise,' I said.

'Thank you. I'm sorry if I—' He broke off and returned to the hectoring manner that seemed to sit so uncomfortably on him. 'You just pass those messages on. Tell them to find her. And tell that bloody woman that I hold her responsible. I thought that I could at least trust her to look after Delia. Now I must go. The worst thing for Delia would be if I were to talk to the police. Good day to you!'

He hurried the few yards to the door and slammed it behind him. The factory was little more than a box with rooflights and no windows. I opened the door in time to see his car leave the yard.

Sir Peter was the only person who had asked me to keep him posted. I rang his home but he had left for a meeting in Edinburgh. I could have phoned Mrs Thrower at the bank, but she had only asked me to take messages and I was feeling bloody-minded.

Mr Thrower had not seemed to care whether or not I told the police about his visit. I phoned Ian. He listened to about ten words of my report and said that he was coming round immediately. When Ian says 'immediately', he means it. He was at the factory before I had finished checking that the packing-room was putting the right birds into the right bags. He brought with him a beardless youth in constable's uniform. His sergeant, I had heard over the factory grapevine, was conducting enquiries between the school and the factory.

We settled down in the office. Ian was very formal and official and quite unlike a husband. He produced a studio photograph in a plastic envelope. 'Is this the man?'

'That looks like him,' I said. 'The moustache had gone and his hair's black now.'

Ian nodded. 'Tell it all from the beginning,' he said. He gave the constable a second nod, which I guessed meant that the lad was to take notes.

I repeated Mr Thrower's words in as much detail as I could remember, withholding only his suggestion of my name as a password. 'He also flatly denied taking any money,' I finished. I remembered a name that both Sir

Peter and Mr Thrower had let slip. 'I suppose he was referring to Sempylene.'

He looked at me sharply. 'What do you know about Sempylene?' he demanded.

'Sir Peter was in here just before Mr Thrower came,' I said. That may have suggested that I knew more than I did, but it remained true. I have my fair share of curiosity or, according to Dad, rather more than my fair share; and it was high time that Ian learned that he need not expect to keep secrets from his wife for more than a day, if that.

Ian seemed to accept that he could speak more freely. 'In the circumstances, Thrower said pretty much what you'd expect him to say, whether or not he was in on the fiddles. You can stop taking notes,' he added to the constable. 'I'm thinking aloud. The question is, did he really have nothing to do with Delia's disappearance?'

'He struck me as sincere,' I said.

'It could be true. We have a vague report of a teenager getting into a van. But, unless her father was being more devious than I give him credit for, we now know that he's back in a job and that he lives or works within an hour's drive of here.'

'So do a couple of hundred thousand other people,' I pointed out.

'True. I think it's time we got the lawyers to disgorge his present address. Or you could send him that message . . . '

'No,' I said. 'I promised.'

He gave a sigh. 'Fair enough. I have my secrets, so you're entitled to yours. It's a pity you didn't think to get a look at his car.'

'But I did,' I said. It was hard to know what was in Delia's best interests. I was not going to betray any confidences, but Ian might as well benefit from my aid as an ordinary witness. 'I hadn't quite finished my story – or is it a statement? – when you sidetracked me on the subject of the Sempylene takeover.'

The last word was a blind guess, based on no more than a remark by Wallace that most major frauds took place during takeovers, but Ian didn't react. He nodded to the constable again. 'Let's have it,' he said.

'Dark red hatchback,' I said. 'I think it was a Ford.' I quoted the registration number from memory.

'That's more like it,' Ian said with satisfaction. 'When Thrower left home, he left his own car with his wife. Too easily traced, I suppose. If he's using a hireling or a firm's car, we can find him in minutes. Then, if his story stands up, we'll have to give Delia the full treatment.'

'Tomorrow's Saturday,' I said. 'If you want search-parties . . .'

He smiled. For a moment he was the friend and husband instead of the anxious policeman doing difficult duty. 'I'll phone you later,' he said. 'Not that I expect to find a raped and murdered teenager on the outskirts of the town. Anyway, I hope to God that we don't. But if we have to go through the motions, can I count on you to raise the volunteers? You and your family know all the keepers and beaters for miles around,' he added apologetically.

'I already offered. Just pass the word as soon as you can,' I said, 'and give me times and rendezvous points. Anything else?'

'One thing. May I leave it to you to break the news to Mrs Thrower?'

'At that point,' I said, 'I draw the line. Catch her between the bank and here.'

'I was afraid that you'd say that.'

Mrs Thrower did not return to the factory that day and I was left to fetch money from the bank and deal with the pay packets. In the middle of that chore, Ian phoned. 'Thrower seems to be in the clear,' he said. 'He was at work all day yesterday and his ladyfriend is accounted for.'

'He could have had help,' I pointed out.

'He could. He may have hired somebody. We have another witness to the girl being persuaded to enter the van. The boy recognised Delia and gave a very good description of the man who got out of the van. He sounds very much like somebody known to us.'

I felt my stomach do something very peculiar. 'Known to you as a sex offender, or as a kidnapper for hire?' I asked.

He avoided answering. 'We definitely need search-parties,' he said. 'Meet in the Square at eight tomorrow morning.'

I finished the wages and started telephoning.

Three

About seventy searchers turned out in the morning, a motley bag including old and young, mostly male, some expecting the worst, others enjoying a day out. Two estates had cancelled the day's shooting so that keepers, beaters and members could lend their help. The morning was dry but a cutting wind swept down the valley. Winter was on the way. There would be no more trouble with midge bites or blowflies until another summer came around.

Ian was busy co-ordinating other lines of enquiry. He had left his sergeant in charge of the search, a stiff and pompous man who had once alienated me permanently by interrogating me about a twenty-bore shotgun which he wrongly believed to have been used in a post office hold-up. As with Mrs Thrower and myself, Sergeant Ferless clearly thought that he rather than Ian should have had the promotion.

Newton Lauder is a small town, set in a valley between the high moors. Mixed farmland and small woods surround the town, but these soon give way to open moorland. The Sergeant, rightly this time, decided that a single sweep round the whole town, taking most of the day, would be the most certain way to cover the farmland. If this failed, the enormous task of combing the miles of moors would be necessary; but it would take more than a party of volunteers to comb the miles of heather. Helicopters and thermal imagers would be necessary if Delia was still alive and to be found before she was an old lady.

We moved out on foot to the nearest boundary of the town, and there was a long delay while the line strung itself out up the slope to the main road. Grudgingly obeying orders, the Sergeant accepted my advice on the distribution of the available searchers; so the fittest went to the top of the hill, the more experienced had the woods close to the town, the beaters (who were used to working in a line and covering all the ground) and the sprinkling of local police were spaced out among the others. Those with dogs were also scattered but with a bias towards the town end.

I had brought old Sam along. He might not have much mileage left in him, but he could keep going in the colder weather and his nose was still among the best. We were among the group nearest to the houses and at first we were in thick woodland. The first frosts had gilded the leaves and the wind was beginning to fetch them down and sweep them into drifts that could have hidden a small corpse, so that there was no time to look around and chat.

The walkers had been reminded that this was a search and not a pheasant drive, but their dogs had not always got the message. There was some rabbit-chasing and the occasional pheasant burst up from the bushes and whirred away above the treetops. Sometimes a thumbstick would come to a shoulder or a soft voice would say 'Bang!' Thick clumps of rhododendron and alder had to be penetrated while the searchers on the spot, sheltered from the wind, steamed inside their waxproofed coats and messages were passed for the whole line to halt and stand.

We came out at last into open pasture where we could relax and call the dogs to heel. The middle of the line was now struggling across plough while the far end was among the broken ground and gorse-bushes below the main road. For those at the town end, it became a leisurely stroll.

There had been some changing of places in the line in the thicker woodland and I saw that my left-hand neighbour was now Sir Humphrey Peace. I had not seen him since my wedding day. On that occasion I had been very differently dressed; but I was now clad more in the manner in which he had seen me in the shooting field and I was surprised that he seemed either unable or unwilling to recognise me. His manner suggested that, reluctant as he was to slum it among the peasants, on this occasion *noblesse* did definitely *oblige*.

Something had been found at the other end of the line and we all halted while the nearest policeman panted up the slope to see whether it had any possible significance. Sir Humphrey had diverged from his straightest line to a gate through a barbed-wire fence and was only a few yards away. He seemed glad to mop his forehead and to seat himself on the shooting-stick with which he had been prodding hopefully into patches of cover. Common courtesy required that I speak to him, so I wished him a good morning.

In boots and trousers and an old shooting coat I was perhaps less than ladylike while he was very dapper in a soft tweed jacket and breeches, a club tie at the neck of his checked shirt and very expensive boots. He looked at me as though I had risen out of a cowpat, and returned my greeting without any great warmth.

'I hear that you cancelled your shoot today,' I said.

He shrugged. 'The birds will still be around next week.'

'All the same, it'll be appreciated.'

He looked at his watch. 'I'll probably have to leave at lunchtime,' he said.

'If we stick to the town end of the line, the afternoon will be easier,' I said helpfully.

'I do have other calls on my time,' he said and he looked away towards the hills. Apparently he resented any suggestion that he was less fit than his own keepers and beaters.

We moved on for a hundred yards and stopped again. Two small helicopters were already scouring the moor beyond the main road. When I looked towards their clatter, I saw that Wallace James, Dad's partner, was fifty yards to my right. I changed places with the intervening searcher, a lady from the dog club with a pair of spaniels, and walked over to meet Wal.

'Dad's minding the shop, is he?' I asked.

'I hope so,' Wal said. 'If he hasn't handed over to the first passer-by and gone off on some ploy of his own. He's supposed to come out at lunchtime and I'll go back to the shop.'

I accepted the slur on my father. Even at an age which seemed, to me in my early twenties, to be almost senile, Dad had enough zest in life to seem totally irresponsible. Wallace understood and envied him without approving. 'I'd have expected to see Sir Peter,' I said. 'He hates to miss a bit of excitement.'

'He had a meeting in Edinburgh.'

I was still resenting the pitiful attempts of my friends and family to keep me in the dark. The occasion seemed propitious for digging a little more. 'If it's about the

Sempylene business,' I said, 'I'm surprised that he didn't take you with him.'

Wallace's eyes popped and he made a faint shushing sound and a silencing gesture. He moved closer, seeming to look past my shoulder. 'Keep your voice down,' he said in what was barely more than a whisper. 'I forgot how thick you are with the old boy.'

'So are you,' I said. 'Why didn't he take you along. Is it too confidential for us peasants?'

That needled him, as I intended. 'Nothing like that. He usually likes to have me along to interpret the figures and translate the jargon into basic English. All the accountants in the world seem to be working on this one. Board of Trade, Fraud Squad, you name it, along with the firm's own Finance Department. They form a clique. Plus the fact that the financial whizz-kids resented it when Sir Peter, who was a non-financial director, was kicked up into the chairmanship. So they try to talk verbal shorthand and blind him with technicalities. It gives them a giggle to force him to ask elementary questions so that they can look patient and explain in words of one syllable. But today's meeting is legal and procedural and he can give as good as he gets in that quarter. Believe me,' Wallace said reverently, 'he'll be taking no prisoners today.'

'And how's it coming along?' I asked. Just a friendly, social enquiry.

Wal shrugged. 'We're getting there,' he said. 'So far, no evidence of sweeteners. Just buying with inside knowledge.'

'That's serious enough, isn't it?' I suggested.

'Very serious, very common and very difficult to prove if they've used nominees. It probably wouldn't have come

47

to light at all if their chief financial cook and bottle-washer hadn't done a vanishing act. Now they're having to check out every purchaser for connection with those in the know. Not a word to anybody,' he added seriously. 'If this gets out before we're ready there'll be a financial crash and thousands of jobs up the spout. That's what Sir Peter was put in for, to try and save the jobs.'

'I won't tell anybody,' I promised.

The line moved on. In the extraordinary way in which a body of people always knows more than the sum of the knowledge of its individuals, it was understood that nothing useful had been found. By twelve thirty we had converged on the road to the south of the town. Everybody had brought sandwiches, but a van was waiting in the mouth of a farm-road with soup, tea, coffee and beer – Sir Peter's doing, I discovered later.

Wal took his meal at the roadside while watching the road. I trod down some nettles, spread a plastic bag, sat down on the verge beside him and shared my sandwiches with old Sam.

'What did you think of my figures?' I asked Wal.

He thought it over for a minute. 'All right,' he said at last.

'The supermarket chains are sitting up and taking notice,' I said. 'And, according to Sir Peter, we could sign up most of the shoots if we set about it. We could be a lot bigger. But that would mean bigger premises, refrigerated vans and so on.'

'I wondered how long it would be before that idea took hold,' Wal said. 'I don't know. A lot of small, local operations might be more economic than one big one. Leave it with me.'

I was content. Those words meant that Wal would, in the course of time, produce a beautifully costed feasibility study and let me claim most of the credit. I gave Sam half of another sandwich.

'If you give him food now, he'll be too lazy to work this afternoon,' Wal said. 'Not that it'll matter, probably.'

He could have been suggesting that Sam was too old to be of much help, but I thought not. 'You don't think we're going to find her? Or anything?' I suggested.

Wal looked round but there was nobody nearby. 'It seems unlikely.'

'You think she's with her father?'

'Either that, or she's been taken in order to shut his mouth.'

Quickly, I sifted through what I knew and found a little more of the pattern. 'Of course, that must be it,' I said. 'I just hadn't thought of it that way round. His evidence would be important, wouldn't it?'

'Vital,' Wal said. 'It was his disappearance that really started the alarm bells ringing. We still don't know whether he accidentally chose the most delicate moment to elope or whether he took fright at what was going on. We don't even know how much he knew about it. But the dates are critical. Many of the firm's records have vanished. If he didn't take them with him, as the firm's senior accountant he's the only person who can be categorical as to who knew what when.'

'I think you're right,' I said.

'Here's your father coming,' Wal said. 'I'll leave you to your country stroll. It has to be done. It'd be too damnable if it turned out later that she'd been lying in a coma somewhere near here.' He paused and looked at

49

me with anxious eyes. 'I think you should steer clear of Sir Humphrey. If he speaks to you during the afternoon, stick to the weather.'

Dad arrived beside us before I could ask him what Sir Humphrey had to do with it. Wal took over the jeep and headed back to open the shop. He could have omitted his final warning. Sir Humphrey was speaking on a cordless telephone and soon afterwards a large and glossy car collected him and swept him away.

My father sat beside me. 'Any luck this morning?'

'Not to my knowledge,' I said. 'Some bits and pieces have been collected but I suppose it'll take time to find out whether any of them are relevant. I mean, it's not unknown for a pair of knickers to be left behind in the woods.'

'I just hope that none of them can be traced back to you,' he said. Since I got married he felt free to make that sort of joke.

'If they can, I didn't leave them there,' I said. 'I'm too thrifty. I get it from you. Dad, when did the Sempylene takeover happen?'

'So Ian's been talking freely! I wondered how long it would be before he found out how impossible it is to keep you in the dark. It was while you were on your honeymoon.'

We moved off before I could think of any more questions that might add to my knowledge without revealing how very little I knew.

Apart from the excitement when one of the younger searchers became fascinated with the frogmen who were scouring the bed of the canal, got too close and fell in, the afternoon passed without incident. I stayed next to Dad, but either he knew less than I did about Mr Thrower and Sempylene or else he was guarding his tongue carefully. We came round the northern extremity of the town. The further end of the search reached almost as far as Briesland House and in the distance I saw Mum attach herself to the line. I found myself beside Mum's brother for a while, but Uncle Ronnie seemed to know less than nothing, which was about par for the course. If it doesn't swim or fly or grow antlers, it is of no importance to him and he refuses to waste mental energy on it.

We finished where we had started and were gathered together for a rather stilted word of thanks from the Sergeant. One of the officers brought me a message, relayed over the radio, to say that Ian had been called into Edinburgh.

Dad swept us off for a meal in the pub, which suited me very well. I was in no hurry to get home. I had no fancy to make a meal for one and I had a hunch that I would have time to myself next day.

My hunch proved correct. Ian was out for most of the Sunday. Occasional messages, relayed from different places and promising ever later times for his return home, suggested that he was chasing down scraps of information. Once he phoned from Edinburgh and I guessed that he was keeping his superiors well posted.

I kept my curiosity at bay until I had caught up with the week's housework. When the flat was thoroughly cleaned, Sam had been walked, the laundry was tumble-drying and preparations had been made for our one good meal of the week that evening, I dug into the collection of old newspapers. Ian, who insists on keeping abreast of the world's news, had allowed the delivery of his daily paper to be continued during our only too brief absence. Between my sudden change of status and residence and the distraction of starting a new venture, I had missed the intervening paper collections and the space beneath the stair to the flat above was becoming full of neatly stacked columns of newsprint. Luckily for me, they remained in approximate order of date.

If the result of my search was not very informative, at least it spurred me, after clipping out all references to Sempylene, into tying the papers up into bundles and putting them outside for the next collection which was almost due. The council's men would probably have to send for another van, but that was their problem. The sudden void under the stairs enabled me to stow away some boxes containing wedding presents that I rather hoped never to see again.

I ate a snack for lunch, did the ironing, walked Sam again and then sat down for a read that would have been about as interesting as the story of somebody else's operation if it had not been linked to the disappearance of somebody I knew. The image of Delia in the hands of strangers kept coming between me and the page. I could recall the feelings of menace and doubt. Sam put his head on my knee and I took comfort from rubbing his sleek hide.

Never having had enough money to worry about, I had paid little heed to the financial pages and had missed the first hints that the fall in Sempylene shares reflected serious financial problems in the company. I vaguely remembered an article in the body of the local paper which pointed out the scale of job losses if Sempylene folded but had not paid it much attention. Scottish papers tend to be preoccupied with gloom and doom. Moreover, the article had come out during the hectic run-up to my wedding and I had passed it by, thinking only that its message had been too obvious to be worth printing. The works, which produced hi-tech plastic extrusions for almost the whole spectrum of industries, was to the south of Edinburgh and within car-sharing distance of Newton Lauder. Several of the workers in the defunct poultry and meat pie factories had found work there and had had to be coaxed back.

I made myself a pot of tea and read on. The crunch had come while Ian and I were airbourne for Cyprus. The imminent collapse of Sempylene leaked out. Subsequent articles blamed this on the cancellation of a huge contract for the defence industry. The Government, after being accused of extravagance by the Opposition and pressed to retrench, had, as usual, been as heavily criticised for the effects of its efforts to economise.

The bad news was followed almost immediately by the good. Levieux et Cie, a company vast in Europe but with only a token British presence in Clydebank, had stepped in with an offer to take over Sempylene. The prompt agreement of the Monopolies Commission and the Board of Trade suggested that the takeover had been in the wind for some time. Sir Humphrey Peace, the chairman, had made vague but reassuring statements about job security which had caused panic in the ranks of the unions. I turned to the back page. Sempylene shares, after being virtually given away with a pound of tea, had surged back to near their previous level.

The story had then died the death for some weeks, apart from some editorial chest-thumping on the subject of British defence technology leaking abroad at bargain prices. Then – I looked at the date of the paper and it was only ten days old – there was a brief announcement that Sir Humphrey was retiring on the grounds of health. If Sir Peter's appointment in his place was formally announced, I must have missed it.

The only other item was just two days old and had been reprinted from *The Financial Times*. A press conference, at which the successful conclusion of the takeover was to have been announced, was postponed indefinitely and with no reason given. Nobody was prepared to make any kind of statement. There was some speculation as to whether the French had backed out of the deal, but there was a total lack of facts and the journalist was obviously making bricks without straw. He might well have detected a strong smell of fish, but the threat of libel would have restrained the paper from voicing any suspicions until there was a 'reliable source' to be blamed.

I put the clippings away in an old envelope, fed Sam and decided to do a little gardening and then tidy the garage while I thought about it. Monotonous toil always seems to stimulate my thinking processes. But I had not got much further than to reflect that Sir Humphrey had seemed passably fit when I had seen him the previous day when I was called indoors by the phone. Another message from Ian. He would be home in an hour.

Where had the day gone? Daylight seemed to have slipped away unobserved while I was trying to restore order to the accumulation of odds and ends that Ian had retained in the garage in case they might come in handy some day and had later heaped against the back wall to make room for the new car. I forgot about Sempylene and even Delia and did a quick network diagram in my head to determine how on earth I could get the meal ready for the table and still manage time for a shower and to tart myself up into the sort of wife to whom Ian would find it a pleasure to return.

If Ian had taken the hour he had promised me, I would have made it with time in hand. As it was, he short-changed me by nearly twenty minutes.

I intended to amaze him with my preparedness. As it turned out, I think that he was as surprised as I was. I never heard him come in. I had had my shower but had interrupted my first attempts to get dressed in order to dash through the flat and turn down the potatoes, when I was grabbed from behind by what seemed to be several pairs of hands but turned out to be those of Ian alone. I recognised them just in time to stop myself poking his eye out.

His usual homecoming kiss was more fervent than usual but he was prickly and smelled of sweat. His gingery colouring never showed stubble but his chin became like sandpaper after a few hours. 'You've just got time for a shower and a shave before the meal's ready,' I said, trying, not too hard, to wriggle out of his grasp.

'I'll make a deal with you,' he said. 'I'll shave and shower if you'll come to table just like that.'

'You're turning into a dirty young man,' I told him. 'Not that I'm complaining. But Uncle Ronnie or somebody would be sure to crash in on us. Save yourself up for later.'

'I suppose so.' His grasp slackened.

'It's my turn to bounce all over you,' I said.

He brightened perceptibly and went off to take his shower.

When things were under control in the kitchen I went to

finish dressing. Ian was still under the shower. I spoke to him through the open doors. 'What have you been doing all day?' I asked.

He had water in his ears and I had to repeat the question.

'I think I should leave you guessing,' he said.

'All right then, I'll guess,' I said. I had intended to make one of the flippant guesses which could set us both giggling; but I was still needled by his secretiveness and while I dithered my subconscious fitted a few of my new-found facts together and I decided to make a stab in the dark. 'I think you've been looking for Bernard Thrower,' I said.

He came out of the bathroom in a hurry, towelling his hair. 'Who the hell told you that he'd done another runner?'

'You did, more or less. I must see to the meal,' I said. 'Don't be long.' And I left him to seethe.

The meal was on the table before he came through in slacks and a polo neck, looking very damp and cuddly. The living-cum-dining-room was cosy, with a fire burning and the lighting low.

Instead of putting me through an immediate interrogation, Ian filled his mouth several times in quick succession. He tried not to let me see how much he was enjoying it, because I get angry when he goes through the day without stopping for lunch or even a hot dog, but he couldn't prevent little sounds of pleasure escaping. One of the perks of my job was that I could buy pheasants at wholesale prices, but we only indulged at weekends. Even if there had been time for luxury meals during the week, a diet of roast pheasant would eventually have palled.

When the immediate hunger-pangs had been dulled

he said, 'Now, tell me who's been talking out of turn.'

I waited until he had filled his mouth again. 'You're the detective,' I said. 'But I bet you can't find out.'

He chomped hastily for a few seconds and then swallowed his mouthful almost whole. 'Be serious,' he said. 'I suppose you didn't warn Thrower that I was on his track?'

'How could I?' I asked.

'You knew that I had his car number.'

'That was the only number I had. He didn't leave me his phone number as well.'

He tried out the disbelieving look which might have worked on a prisoner with a guilty conscience. When he found that it did not work on a wife, he said, 'All right, then. How did you know that Thrower had done another bunk?'

I shrugged. 'It seemed obvious,' I said. 'For one thing, it's what he would do. For another, your Control Room's too used to doing things by the book. When they pass on a message they give the time and the place of origin. You've been dashing all over the region like a dog after a rat. So, instead of tracing Mr Thrower through his hire-car and settling down for a nice, cosy interrogation, you've had to follow up every suspected sighting of him.'

Ian's look went from disbelieving to pained. 'What on earth did you mean . . . "It's what he would do"?' he demanded.

I was beginning to enjoy myself. 'His daughter had been taken, to put pressure on him not to talk to you. He'd come out of hiding – only for a few minutes, but for long enough to attract attention.'

'Go on,' Ian said. 'Tell me why you're so sure.'

57

'You didn't believe that it was a sex crime, even after getting a description of the man who seems to have swept Delia off. So he was a professional thug hired for the job. I believed her father when he said that he'd had nothing to do with it. I spoke to Mum and she's had Mrs T hanging round all day. If there'd been a ransom demand I'd have heard about it.'

I got up to serve a tart made with surplus apples from Dad's garden and to bring coffee.

'So what does that leave?' Ian asked me.

'You know perfectly well,' I said.

'I do. I want to know how much you know that you shouldn't.'

'It only adds up one way. Mr Thrower was a key figure during the run-up to the takeover of Sempylene by Levieux.' Ian looked at me very hard but waited for me to go on. 'It was in the papers,' I pointed out. 'If the authorities have detected a lot of buying before the rise, by Sempylene directors or people who could be connected to them, Mr Thrower would be one of the few people who could state whether the dates of those purchases were before or after the buyers could have known that the takeover was coming. There's no crime in making a good guess before the privileged knowledge actually arrived.

'The others who knew about the dates would be the directors themselves, especially Sir Humphrey Peace as chairman. But, as he seems to have resigned under rather a cloud, I assume that he's under suspicion with the others, so he's hardly likely to be helpful. Obviously the correspondence files didn't help or there wouldn't be all this fuss. Can't you get the dates from Levieux?'

Ian hesitated, pouring himself a glass of wine. One of

the surprises in our relationship had been to find that he enjoyed a glass of wine, but only of a quality that our slender budget could rarely run to. It happens, however, that almost my only talent, apart from clay-shooting and being able to whistle through my teeth, is an ability to get the utmost out of the kits of winemaking concentrates now available. There are usually a couple of demijohns blooping away in the airing cupboard and several more settling in the cool of the former coalshed. Fussy as he is about wines, Ian seems to appreciate my efforts. That may not be why he married me, but I sometimes think that it is why he will never leave.

He took some wine, rolled it around his tongue and swallowed gratefully. 'This is your best batch yet,' he said. 'I hope you can remember how you did it.' He seemed to decide that I knew so much that a little more would not hurt. 'Levieux are being very unhelpful and, of course, they're mostly outside our jurisdiction. Their local executives know nothing, or that's what they say.'

'In other words,' I said, 'they were also cutting themselves a piece of cake. Right?'

'That seems possible,' Ian admitted.

'My guess would be that Mr Thrower saw what was going on. He took fright and did a bunk and then Sir Humphrey, or some other director, or a syndicate of the whole bally lot of them, hired somebody to kidnap Delia, to make sure that Mr Thrower keeps his head down until the shit's stopped flying – if you'll pardon my French.'

Ian held his glass up to the light and then went through the rigmarole again. 'That's pretty much how we see it,' he said at last. 'I'll find out who's been spilling the beans, but I must admit that it's a relief to be able to talk about it.

We disagree on one or two points. You're assuming that Mr Thrower wasn't in it from the first. We think that he was in with the others. You seem to assume that when the investigation started he felt endangered. We think that he just plain ran off with his ladyfriend.'

I gathered up the dishes and we went through to the kitchen.

'You see,' Ian said. 'Nobody came to disturb us.'

'Sorry if I disappointed you,' I said. 'But they would have done. It's what Dad calls Sod's Law.'

'Your father blames Sod's Law for a lot of things.'

I washed while Ian dried. 'What you said didn't quite make sense,' I told him. 'It was Mr Thrower's disappearance that first attracted attention to the goings-on. He wouldn't have risked that if he was involved. And a man who's making an illicit bob on the stock market might elope but he isn't in a good position to change identities and disappear for good. Have you tracked any dealings back to him?'

'Not yet. His girlfriend's aunts and cousins are being checked out now.'

'Did she vanish with him?' I asked.

'Not the second time. She's still hanging around their love-nest, worried sick. When he heard about the kidnapping, he seems to have dashed through here to protest his non-involvement and then did his second disappearing act. She's promised to get in touch with me if she hears from him, on the understanding that we'll protect both of them and keep it confidential. She may even do it. I gave her this address and phone number.'

I nearly dropped a glass. 'What on earth did you do that for?'

'She doesn't know that I live here. Thrower phoned her and he told her that the factory manager was the one person he thought he could trust. She asked me if I knew where you lived. I thought that she might be more likely to contact another woman and a potential ally than the police.

'She didn't want to contact a police station. Understandably. If her lover surfaces, somebody might well decide that it would be surer and cheaper to have him knocked off than to go on holding his daughter indefinitely. And the cop-shop may be watched. There are those who have a lot of friends around here.'

'Sir Humphrey?' I suggested.

Ian threw up his hands in horror, putting one of my best plates at risk. 'Don't even say it aloud. Unless some new evidence turns up, he could sue the hell out of both of us. You're not supposed to know any of this,' he said seriously, 'and nobody would believe that you didn't get it from me. So if you repeat a single word that we've said in here, I swear to God I'll have grounds for divorce. Until that day,' Ian said, with a complete change of tone and hanging the dish-towel over the rail, 'we are still man and wife and I'm legally entitled to do . . . this!'

He made a grab at me and I fled in the general direction of the bedroom.

Four

Reporters must have been poking around in Newton Lauder during my quiet day at home, because Monday's papers were full of the kidnapping story. None of them had so far made a connection with the Sempylene takeover. Either they had been misdirected by the fact that the frauds were being handled from Edinburgh while the kidnapping was left to Ian in Newton Lauder, hindered or helped by any advice that he cared to call for; or else the police had had the sense to keep that aspect out of print for the sake of Delia's life. All the same, it seemed a nuisance and an invasion of privacy, with Ian's name and quotations from his brief statements all over the front pages and even a photograph that made him look like the sort of policeman to be avoided on a dark night.

At least I was spared the presence of Mrs Thrower, simultaneously anxious and disapproving. Mum phoned to say that Mrs T felt unable to return to work just yet, if ever, phrasing it in terms of apology which I am sure were her own. Knowing Mum, I could guess that Mrs Thrower had been moved into my old bedroom. She was certainly not at home. The few reporters who arrived at the factory in the hope of a few agonised quotes from a distraught mother were sent packing.

As it happened, a bright teenager with a certificate in typing and book-keeping had applied for a factory job. I shot her straight into the secretary's chair with a promise that the desk would be hers if she proved herself and a mental promise to myself that Mrs Thrower would come back to the office over somebody's dead body – preferably her own, if that were physically possible. I was sorry for the woman, but that didn't make her combination of arrogance and an air of patronage any easier to bear.

Young Samantha turned out to be a gem. Efficiency and morale both rose to previously impossible heights. By the Monday evening she had mastered the filing and invoicing systems and had even developed enough confidence to make my phone-calls for me, leaving me free for a blitz on the factory workings.

I decided to give Mrs Thrower a powerful hint by taking her the few personal odds and ends that she had left in the secretary's desk. The shop had already closed but Ian was still too busy to chauffeur me out to my old home. When I said that I would walk to Briesland House and he could cook his own meal, he capitulated at last and met me in the police car park with the keys to the car and a solemn warning that if I put just one scratch on its lovingly polished paintwork he would personally prosecute me for dangerous driving.

Whether he would really have taken such drastic action remains uncertain, but it was nearly put to the test. I was turning into the by-road and paying careful attention to my signals – Dad blames Sod's Law for the fact that nobody ever has two successive cars with the indicator control on the same side – when a brilliant light came rushing at me. Blinded, I could only stamp on the brakes. There was a blast of sound, the light went by and a motorbike was tearing away towards the junction with the main Edinburgh road, leaving me sitting shaking in a stalled car.

After ten deep breaths, I had recovered enough to drive shakily up to the front of Briesland House. The outside light was on and I walked once round the car. I was amazed to find that, as far as I could make out in the unsatisfactory light, I was still scratch-free and immune to prosecution. The by-road had always seemed to me to be barely wide enough to accept a car. I blessed the rider for his skill if not for his manners.

Footsteps were approaching, coming along the by-road from the direction of the house that Mrs Thrower had rented. They turned in at the drive. There was something about the uneven rhythm of them that made me uneasy.

I turned to the front door just as Mum opened it. 'I heard a car,' she said. 'Is Ian letting you play with his new toy—?'

She broke off as Mrs Thrower came stumbling into the puddle of light. Her hair and her hands were all over the place and her whole manner was distraught. 'That man . . . ' she gasped. 'That man . . . '

Mum is always at her best in a crisis. I would have let Mrs Thrower babble out her story on the doorstep, but Mum had her indoors and sitting in a deep chair with a brandy in her hand in a matter of seconds. 'Now,' she said, 'tell us what's happened.'

Mrs Thrower took a gulp of brandy and choked. We waited. 'There was a man,' she said hoarsely at last.

'We gathered that,' Mum said. 'What did he do? Start from the beginning. You went round to your house to fetch something.'

64

'He must have been waiting, in the darkness,' Mrs Thrower said. She gave a ladylike shudder. 'When I opened the door and switched the lights on, he appeared suddenly behind me and pushed inside. He was awful, horrible!'

She swallowed the rest of the brandy. She was too ladylike to ask for more, but she sat looking at the empty glass. Mum took the hint and filled it for her.

'But are you hurt?' I asked her.

'Yes. No, not really. Not to say hurt. He . . . he pushed me, more than once. He was a nasty, weaselly man with . . . Would you understand if I said that he had hot eyes?'

Mum and I both said yes.

'He wanted to know whether Bernard knew that Delia had been kidnapped and I told him that he did. Then he said to tell Bernard that he'd better keep his mouth shut or awful things would happen to Delia.' Mrs Thrower dabbed at her eyes and sipped from her glass again. 'I said that I wasn't in touch with Bernard and he said that I'd better get in touch with him if I wanted to see Delia again.'

'We'd better phone Ian,' I said.

'No!' Mrs Thrower flung the word out in a squawk that made me jump. 'He said not to go to the police or they'd do those things to Delia, and to me as well.'

'Don't upset yourself,' Mum said. 'Finish your brandy and I'll make a cup of tea.' I thought that she was going to tell Mrs Thrower to go and wash her face in cold water, but instead she went on, 'Deborah can tell Ian what you've said. He'll know what to do for the best. Tomorrow, he'll make some arrangement to smuggle you into the police building, to look at photographs or make up an Identikit or whatever they do.'

After a little more coaxing and reassurance and some more brandy, Mrs Thrower calmed down slightly and agreed that that would be best. The brandy was having its effect and her appearance was made tipsier by her untidy hair. 'I shan't be coming back to work,' she told me. 'I just couldn't face it any more. I'm sorry to let you down, but I'm sure you'll manage somehow.'

I said that I was sure I would and made my escape, leaving the oddments from her desk on the hall table.

Ian walked twice around the car, inspecting it for damage, before he would let me tell him about Mrs Thrower's visitor. Then he was ready to listen. 'Was that the same man who was seen collecting Delia?' I asked him.

'No.'

'But you recognise the description?'

'Not for sure. I'll find out tomorrow.'

'At least you're finding out who they are.'

'I'd much rather know *where* they are,' he said.

Three days slipped away.

Ian was still torn between police discipline and a need to discuss his problems with me. He compromised by discussing only those matters which he thought I already knew but, by piecing together the fragments that remained unsaid, I gathered that Mrs Thrower had made an identification of her visitor from a photograph but that the twin searches for her husband and daughter were bogged down. Bernard Thrower, Ian said, had returned his hired car to the hirers, accepted a lift to the nearest railway station and taken a ticket to Edinburgh Waverley. From there, as Ian pointed out, he could have gone on to Glasgow or Dundee, or even London, to hire another car from some small operator and, if he so wished, could return by road. He was certainly lying very low. Of Delia and her kidnappers, and of the kidnappers' known associates, there was no sign at all. An application to tap the phone-lines of the directors of Sempylene had been turned down. Mr Thrower's ladyfriend was being monitored strictly – by women detectives, Ian assured me primly, as though I suspected him of hiding in her bathroom cupboard – but there had been no sign of contact.

On the Thursday evening, the whole case stood on its head.

Ian had once again been in Edinburgh for discussion, implied criticism and a general directive to do something clever for God's sake, but he had phoned to say that he was back in his office and would be home in an hour. He sounded depressed.

I was trying to do everything at once, including catching up with the day's news – which meant turning up the television (Ian's) above the noises of the washing machine (a wedding present from Sir Peter), the kettle (ditto from Uncle Ron) and the cyclotherm oven (Wallace and Janet) – so that I almost failed to hear the sound of the doorbell.

When I got to the door, a slim, natural blonde in her thirties was on the step.

Nature favoured me with robust good health and enough strength and stamina to keep up with the men of my family in their thousand and one outdoor pursuits. I wouldn't have it any other way. I would not want to be fragile, but there are times when I would love to have that often deceptive air of fragility that some women have and which makes men want to wrap them in cotton wool and cuddle them. This woman looked as though a breeze would send her bowling along the street and an unkind word would put her into shock. She wore heavy waterproofs and no make-up and her blonde hair, which showed signs of having been well styled in the not too distant past, had been pressed flat and then combed out, apparently by the use of fingers but, even so, she looked sexier than I do at my best. It was dark outside but her eyes, as near as I could tell under the lamp, seemed to be blue. They would be. There was a motor-scooter parked at the kerb.

'I'm Elaine Anderton.'

She said it as though I should know the name but it meant nothing to me. For a frantic moment I tried to place her as a friend of a friend, behind counters, on a stool in the local pub or as the secretary of one of our business contacts. Surely she couldn't be a policewoman? Not even a ten-year-old vandal would come along quietly with somebody so obviously incapable of violent activity.

'Should I know the name?' I asked carefully.

'Oh. I thought you would. Bernard said . . . ' Her voice, which was tremolo, suggesting tears not far away, tailed off.

'Bernard Thrower? You're his . . . ?' My voice did the same while I tried to choose the least offensive synonym for 'mistress'.

'Yes. Bernard phoned me after he'd come to see you. He said that I should contact you if I didn't know what to do. He said you were the only person he'd met that he thought he could trust.'

'Did he, indeed?' I thought that Bernard must have picked on me because I was fresh in his harassed mind; or else he'd gone out of it. But perhaps, if he was more devious than I gave him credit for, his suggestion of a message and a password had been a trap which I had avoided. 'You'd better come inside.'

She followed me in, clumsily. I put her clumsiness down to the thick waterproofs and helped her out of them. She stood still like a child being undressed, still speaking. 'There were people watching me, but I think they were the police. I only had to slip out the back way. It was easy. That's the way the man came in. I keep my scooter in a shed at the back, and there's a lane.'

The blast of sound through the open-plan flat did nothing for her look of desperation or mine. I turned my wedding presents down or off and led her across the dividing line into the living-room.

'Do sit down,' I said. 'What man?'

She was too distraught to hear me. 'A man came to the back door. He just walked straight in without a knock or a by-your-leave. He slapped me. Here.' She pointed to her left cheek. 'Is there a mark?'

I assured her that her beauty was still unblemished.

'He told me that Delia would never be seen again if Bernie or I talked to the police. And he said that he'd come back and cut my face up if I told them that he'd been there. He really did have a razor. He showed it to me.' She made a nervous gesture that nearly knocked over the standard lamp. 'I don't even know your name,' she added. 'Bernard just called you the factory manager.'

Did she know that I was the wife of the investigating officer? If she didn't know my name, obviously not. 'Call me Deborah,' I said. 'And do sit down. You've heard from Mr Thrower?'

She turned towards me and her skirt swept an ornament off the coffee table. 'Only twice since he came to see you.

69

He phoned me in an awful hurry. He said that Delia had been kidnapped and everything was going to go mad and he'd have to go even deeper into hiding for a bit. And—'

I had had a long day and my feet were tired. Manners prevented me from sitting down while a guest was standing. Silly, but that was the way I had been brought up. 'Sit down,' I said firmly.

'And he said—'

There was a chair just behind her. I gave her a gentle push and she sat down. I don't think that she even noticed. I dropped thankfully into another chair.

'And Bernie said that Delia would be in great danger if the police found him and they'd certainly be watching me so he might not be able to contact me direct.' She took a deep breath. 'He phoned once more and said that you were the only person who'd seemed to be sympathetic and he thought he could trust you and that if all else failed we could keep in touch through you. Have you heard from him again?'

'Not a word.'

'I don't know what to do,' she said. She looked at me like a spaniel awaiting a hand-signal. Real tears were beginning to overflow her lower lids.

'What did this man look like?' I asked. 'The one who threatened you.'

'Scruffy.'

'But apart from that?'

'Very ordinary. He didn't sound ordinary, he sounded hard. But he looked as if you could pass him in the street without really seeing him.'

Not the weaselly man with hot eyes, then.

It seemed that not only men were vulnerable to that air

of ethereal helplessness. 'Calm down and try to relax,' I advised her. 'Have you had anything to eat?'

'Yes, I think so. Yes,' she said more positively. 'I stopped at a café to ask the way here and while I was making up my mind what to say I had something. I can't remember what.'

'That's all right then. I'm going to give you a drink and when you're feeling better we'll decide what to do.' In my ears, my voice sounded very like Mum's. I nearly told her to go and wash her face in cold water.

While I made inroads into the remains of our duty-free supplies, I thought frantically. The absent Mr Thrower might trust me but I had never asked him to do so. Nor had I given him any promises. My first duty was to Ian and Ian was not the sort of officer who would crash in and make things worse. And he would know what to do. I made up my mind.

There was a telephone extension in the bedroom but if I used it she would hear the main instrument clicking and she might even listen in. Our next-door neighbours were away and had left the key with me.

Still following Mum's example, I gave her brandy, slightly diluted. 'I have to go out for a minute,' I said. 'You drink this, and when I get back we'll do some serious thinking.'

'All right,' she said. She seemed very trusting.

I dashed next door through a thin drizzle and let myself in. The time-switch had lit a lamp and switched on a small transistor radio. I turned the radio down and dialled. The desk put me through to Ian's extension.

'Bernard Thrower's girlfriend's just turned up at the flat,' I said as soon as I heard Ian come on the line. 'She's in a bit of a state, not having heard from him and not knowing what's going on. And she's had a man at the door, just like Mrs Thrower. Did you know that?'

'I didn't even know that she'd left home,' Ian said. 'I suppose those WPCs were powdering their blasted noses.'

'Don't be sexist,' I told him. 'Even men have to go and spend a penny now and again. And she came out the back way, she said. I suppose the kidnappers can't get hold of Mr Thrower and they want to be sure that he connects Delia's kidnapping with his silence. Anyway, Mr Thrower told her that he might have to keep in touch through "the factory manager". Just as you said, he seems to have decided that I'm trustworthy. Perhaps it's time that you did the same.'

There was a silence on the line. I was about to ask if he was still there when he spoke suddenly. 'I was just going to phone you,' he said. 'A message came in a few minutes ago. Bernard Thrower's turned up. He's in the local emergency ward, but I think he'll be transferred to Edinburgh. He was in a car smash.'

'Is it bad?' I asked.

'Very bad, from what I hear.'

'How did it happen?' I was wondering whether he'd been run off the road.

'Mischance,' Ian said. 'A Panda car was doddling along a minor road, minding its own business. He seems to have seen it behind him and thought that it was after him and panicked. He put his boot down and arrived at a bend faster than anybody could have got round it. That was this morning. He wasn't carrying any identification and we were only alerted to who he was when he woke up for a few seconds and asked to see you.'

'By name?'

'By job description. He probably wants you to transmit reassuring messages.'

Some most unpleasant ideas were occurring to me. 'I presume you're keeping this very quiet,' I said.

Ian was ahead of me. 'God, yes! We can't take chances with his daughter's life.' There was another pause. I could almost hear him scratching the stubble on his neck, his habit when deep in thought. 'When he goes in to Edinburgh he'll go into surgery for hours and hours and then be dopey for hours more,' Ian said at last. 'I want to get as much as I can before they shift him – if he ever does come to again. Sergeant Ferless is sitting with him for the moment but I'm just off to join them. How trustworthy do you want to be?'

'Very,' I said, wondering what I was letting myself in for.

'Could you break the news to the lady and then bring her to the hospital?'

There are those who seem to enjoy breaking bad news, but I hate it. I wanted to protest, but I could see that I had brought the duty on myself. 'You've got the car,' I said, 'and she only has a scooter.'

'Take a taxi.'

'Send one for me.' I could be just as peremptory as he could, on a good day. 'Not a police car, mind, or she'll have seven fits.'

I hung up, re-started the radio and locked up carefully.

In a certain kind of novel to which I am addicted, I would have returned home to find that she had either vanished or was now lying on my bed, probably naked and certainly dead, transfixed by some unlikely weapon. In real life, I

73

found her still in the same chair, dripping tears into the dregs of the brandy.

'Have you thought what we should do?' she asked me hopefully. Evidently I was now the team leader or Brown Owl or something.

I refilled her glass and waited until she had taken another sip. 'I went out to get some news,' I said, 'and I got it. It's not very good. You've got to be brave.'

She put down her glass and looked at me, very white but making an effort. As gently as I could, I told her that her lover was at the hospital, seriously injured.

Surprisingly, her first thought was neither for him nor for herself and my opinion of her went up. 'That poor child!' she said. 'Either way, things don't look good for her. If those men find out, they'll know that they don't need her any more.' She drank some more brandy and put down the empty glass so violently that it skidded across the table and on to the floor. She jumped to her feet. 'I must go to him.'

I picked up the glass and checked it for cracks. 'We'll both go. I've called for a taxi.'

'We don't have to wait for that. We can go on my scooter.'

Even if I had been prepared to ride on a scooter on what was turning out to be a damp night, no way was I going pillion behind a stranger who had absorbed two very large brandies. 'The taxi's on its way,' I said, hoping that it was true. 'Let's get you tidied up for hospital visiting.'

She washed her face and put on a little make-up and then stood while I brushed her hair. I had a feeling that I was making a mistake. She was becoming too damned attractive by half and Ian was always susceptible to pathos in a woman, provided only that she was pretty.

She seemed to have accepted the bad news at face value,

74

but as we were going out to Mr Ledbetter's taxi she pulled back for a moment. 'This isn't some sort of trick?'

'I wish it was,' I said.

That seemed to satisfy her. 'I'd rather that it was,' she said shakily. 'But I suppose that no trick would change anything now.' She stooped to get in. We rode up to the hospital in silence, but she was perched on the edge of the seat and I could feel her willing the taxi onward. The Emergency sign was a beacon among the hospital lights. She darted in through the double doors while I was telling the driver to send the bill to my husband.

I caught her up at the desk. Ian was there, in discussion with a doctor who had once stitched my hand when I sliced it while skinning a rabbit. She was trying to ask several simultaneous questions and not making any of them clear.

Ian snapped something at the doctor. I could only make out the word ' . . . private'. The doctor swept us into a small office. Ms Anderton paused for breath.

'If there's one thing we need it's total confidentiality,' Ian said. 'If reporters come sniffing round—'

'Which they will,' the doctor said gloomily.

'—telling them that he's unidentified will only make them sit up and take notice. Make something up. He's Allan McKay, say, from Inverness. You don't have his address here but his next of kin have been informed. You'll pass it on?'

The doctor nodded and made a note.

Both men returned their attention to Elaine Anderton. She must have guessed that Ian was a policeman but she was past caring. By now, she had found her second wind and a little more coherence. 'I want to see him,' she told the doctor. 'I want to see that he's all right.'

The doctor had had more than a little experience of breaking bad news. He sat down behind the desk, indicated the stacking chairs that were lined along the opposite wall and waited. His power of suggestion was stronger than mine. We sat.

'I'm afraid that's not possible,' he said.

'For one thing,' said Ian, 'we're too late. He's already on the way to Edinburgh by ambulance.'

Ms Anderton tried to jump to her feet. Ian prevented her, by patting her reassuringly on the shoulder and then leaning his weight on her. He and the doctor had both adopted avuncular manners towards her; they also seemed both to prefer that anyone in an agitated state should remain firmly seated.

'Even if you caught up with him,' said the doctor gently, 'you couldn't see him. He'll be in surgery for hours. Are you his wife?' he asked her.

'His fiancée,' she said defiantly.

The doctor apparently knew that the injured man had a wife but he managed not to raise his eyebrows. 'I'm afraid his condition is critical,' he said.

'The crash was a bad one,' Ian said. 'The car rolled over more than once.'

I had decided to say nothing but I changed my mind. 'Surely he must be conscious, if he was trying to get a message to me . . . '

'A few seconds of lucidity,' said the doctor, 'before the intercranial haemorrhage took over.' He paused, weighing his words. 'It's early days,' he said at last, 'but, to be honest, his chances are far from good. Apart from the skull fracture, he's broken more bones than I'd care to list and we suspect a rupture of the spleen. There's also spinal

76

damage. If he recovers consciousness, it certainly won't be before late tomorrow.'

'If? Not when? If?' Elaine Anderton's voice was running away up the scale.

The doctor nodded sadly. I braced myself, ready to help quell an outburst of hysteria, but she took the other escape route. Her eyes rolled up and she fell sideways across my knees. I caught her before she rolled to the floor. There was no weight to her.

The doctor came round the desk quickly, felt her pulse and pulled up an eyelid. 'Shock,' he said. 'Understandable. We'll keep her here overnight under sedation.'

'Private room?' Ian suggested.

'Quite so.'

'I'll fix up somewhere for her to go after that, where she needn't be alone. I'll be in touch tomorrow.'

Ms Anderton was removed, feet first, on a trolley by a nurse and an orderly, with the doctor in attendance. She looked rather as I have always pictured the Lady of Shalott, pathetic and yet glamorous. Similarly placed, I would have been an inert lump of meat.

'The poor kid!' Ian said. 'I'll take you home. Bernard Thrower will be Edinburgh's business now.'

The rain had set in. Usually, Ian would have let me wait in the doorway while he fetched the car. But he was deep in thought and rather than break into it I followed him across an acre of wet tarmac. We were both wet by the time we were in the car, but he sat behind the wheel with the key still in his hand.

'I wish she'd postponed the vapours for a little longer,' he said. 'I wanted to ask her . . . '

'About Mr Thrower's papers?' I suggested.

'We already have those. Her bungalow was searched, quite illegally. No, I wanted her to repeat every word he's said to her.'

'Edinburgh can ask him for themselves,' I said.

'I doubt it. Before you arrived, the doc was saying that he'd be surprised if Thrower even makes it to Edinburgh.'

'Oh dear!' I said inadequately.

'Yes, it's bad. We've got to find that girl before whoever's got her realises that they don't need her any more. And still not a damned thing to go on. The solution of every case depends on getting the breaks and so far they're not coming our way.'

'Something will turn up,' I said.

'That's for sure. Probably the girl's toes, if the luck doesn't turn first.'

Five

Nearly another week slipped away. Mr Thrower, I was given to understand, was still alive, still unconscious and still of doubtful prognosis. The doctors' view, relayed by Ian, was that, if he survived at all, it might be as a human vegetable.

Whatever was happening in the case, I was no longer part of it. Ian had resumed his role of discreet and close-mouthed officer but, from his prolonged absences and the constant trickle of messages which reached him at home, I could guess that intensive searches were continuing for Delia, for witnesses to her kidnapping and for any signs of the suspected kidnappers or their associates.

With Ian determined not to bring his work home, it seemed that my peripheral part in the case had been due to coincidence. Mrs Thrower's work at the factory had brought her husband there and, finding me sympathetic, he had suggested a message which could bring him out of hiding. When no such message had been passed he had decided that I was not in cahoots with the police and had mentioned me to Elaine Anderton – *Miss* Anderton, Ian told me – as a possible message-passer and letter-drop.

Delia's predicament was haunting me, leaping into my mind like a demon out of a trap-door at unexpected moments. But from now on, I thought, I would know little more than I could read in the papers and infer from Ian's movements. And that would be little enough. Somehow, all mention of the accident to Mr Thrower had been suppressed and the kidnapping was yesterday's news.

The fates had other ideas. I must have inherited some of Dad's knack for finding trouble. With him, the knack was mostly a combination of curiosity with antennae ever alert for anything suspicious. He had passed me the gene of curiosity, but the rest seems to be blind chance. There must have been clues to Delia's whereabouts scattered around the countryside, contact traces and fallen tears, but nobody had managed to find them. The tiny clue that came to the factory could so easily have passed through unrecognised. Perhaps something else would have turned up to give the police a lead. One of the many officers might have picked up a whisper about strangers behaving oddly. Or Delia might never have been heard of again. The door-to-door enquiries and the searches which were still being carried out over the moors by helicopter were, as it turned out, in all the wrong places.

We were busy at the factory. Pheasants were full-grown and the commercial shoots were holding their bigger days. (Later in the season, as birds became thinner on the ground, bags would reduce.) And the shoots which had been cancelled on the day of the search had been rescheduled. Pheasants were coming in at such a rate that I was beginning to wonder whether we hadn't bitten off more than we could chew – or more than even our new markets could absorb.

When, in mid-morning, the whirr of the plucking machine died away, I was out of the office in two jumps.

A machinery breakdown we needed like an outbreak of gapeworm. Plucking by hand would be expensive and impossibly slow. The cold-room would be overflowing before help could reach us from the makers. I had been demanding a standby machine for weeks but Sir Peter had been either too busy or too thrifty to sanction it.

I dashed out into the brightly lit preparation-room, ready to do something constructive like tearing my hair and running round in little circles, but it seemed that Madge, who had been operating the noisy machine, had stopped it to hold a discussion. If this was a convening of the shop stewards, the same reaction would have been appropriate.

On the stainless steel table beside the plucking machine a dozen naked pheasants were laid out. On a butcher's block Mrs Beattie, a tireless worker but much too dignified to have a Christian name, had been removing heads, wings and legs, gutting the birds into polythene sacks and laying them out for weighing and sorting by size, all with the effortless speed of a compulsive knitter. She and Madge were stooped over a plucked but otherwise complete pheasant.

I looked where Mrs Beattie's finger pointed. Some birds arrived at the factory with the crop already burst by shot or by impact with the ground. Of the remainder, about one bird in three or four, depending on the operator's handling, came out of the plucking machine with the crop newly opened, spilling grain or rape-seed. Some grain was spilling over the table. I had another moment of panic, thinking that they had spotted something toxic which would result in the whole batch being dumped; but Mrs Beattie was singling out some tiny grains from among the others. I looked more closely.

Two glass beads of an unusual lavender or lilac colour winked under the fluorescent lights.

'Didn't the paper say that Mrs Thrower's wee girl was wearing her bracelet?' Mrs Beattie asked.

I looked at Madge. 'Tell Samantha—' She removed her ear protectors and I began again. 'Tell Samantha to phone. Get a message to my husband that somebody should come down here straight away.'

She nodded and hurried into the office.

'Was this the last bird to come out of the machine?' I asked Mrs Beattie.

Another nod. The ladies soon got used to communicating by signals around the noisy machine. 'It was Melanesian,' she said. She meant melanistic.

The other girls had gathered round, pleased with the excitement and the break in routine. 'It looks just the colour of the bracelet Delia wore,' another girl said.

I was more cautious. 'The colour would look different under the fluorescent lights.'

'It's under these lights that we're used to seeing it,' said Mrs Beattie.

I stood still and used my eyes. Allowing for the different lighting, the colour of the beads looked very like those I had seen on Delia's wrist. There could have been thousands of similar baubles in the neighbourhood but the likelihood of a bracelet or necklace being broken in the woods was more remote. Mrs Thrower had said something about the bracelet having been brought from Turkey; but it might easily have reached Turkey from Birmingham.

One of the pheasant's wings still bore a dark red tag, printed with two digits that could have represented the current year. The remaining feathers looked unusually dark. The spurs were small. I looked in the bag that caught most of the feathers. There was a layer of very dark feathers on top of the contents.

Madge tapped my elbow. 'He's on his way,' she said. She stooped to look again at the beads. 'A wink of light caught my eye or it'd've gone in the bin. I thought to myself, that looks awfu' like the beads Miss Delia showed me that her Dad gave her. You think it's the same?'

'They look very like it,' I said. Between the cold-room door and the plucking machine, another steel table was heaped with pheasants in full feather. 'Did these all come in together?' I asked her.

'They came yesterday,' she said. 'Whether they're all off the same estate I couldno' say.'

'The crops will have to be opened, but we'd better not disturb anything until the police are here.' I looked again at the grain surrounding the two bright beads. 'Would you say that this was barley?'

Mrs Beattie had been brought up on a farm. 'Definitely barley,' she said. 'And look.' I looked. What I had taken to be small shot was some other seed.

'Rape-seed?' I suggested.

'Turnip,' she said. 'They're o'er sma' for rape. Somebody's neips has bolted to seed.'

'Well done,' I said. She looked gratified. 'Now, you girls had better go and help with cleaning and packaging. Tell the others we've had a machinery breakdown.'

'They'll run out in an hour. What'll they dae then?'

'I'll let them know.'

Tyres yelped to a halt in the yard outside. The girls wanted to linger and share in the excitement but I shooed them through the door into the other unit.

Ian came in on the double, but scowling. 'This had better be good,' he said.

I hid my excitement rather than risk raising false hopes. 'You can be the judge,' I told him. I showed him the beads. 'They look exactly like the beads in the bracelet Delia wears,' I said. 'I've never seen others quite that colour. Mr Thrower brought it from Turkey. It may be just a cruel coincidence, but she wore the bracelet around here almost every day and the girls are unanimous. Follow it up or not, just as you like. How are you off for other leads?'

He shook his head impatiently. 'Where did the bird come from?'

'I don't know but I think I can find out. Meantime, I'll want the prep-room working again as soon as possible.'

We snapped at each other for a minute or two. Policemen always think that everything for a hundred yards around a scrap of possible evidence can be left intact for weeks. Others of us know better. We settled on a compromise. Madge would open the crops of the remaining pheasants while somebody came to remove any evidence that might be needed for scientific study. Ian went out to his car to use the radio while I sent Samantha out of the office on some improbable errand.

I waited until Ian joined me. 'Shall I do this by phone?' I asked.

'Tell me what you're doing first.'

'Only two keepers brought pheasants yesterday, but both of them brought more than they'd have shot in a day. Sometimes they save them up for a day or two, damn them! And sometimes they pick up each other's birds to save time and expense. But I can probably pin down where that bird came from.'

84

'How?'

'The bird was a melanistic cock. That's a sort of deformity of coloration, very dark – a genetic throwback. You don't come across them very often. Keepers tend to remember them.'

'If you can narrow it down without starting a lot of gossip, go ahead,' he said. 'What would beads be doing in a pheasant's crop anyway?'

'They pick up grit to help grind up the other stuff,' I explained. 'Especially hard grain. I suppose a small glass bead would function very well. If the stringing broke while she was being manhandled . . . ' I stopped. For a moment my voice refused to work.

'I understand,' Ian said. 'Get on with it.'

I looked up numbers. One of the keepers was near his home. His wife fetched him from the shed. He said that he hadn't seen a melanistic bird all year. He wanted to know why I was asking and I told him that I was damned if I was paying for a bird that had been shot from all directions and at close range and was carrying more shot than its own body-weight. He sounded amused.

The other keeper was away from home but was expected back in about an hour. He had collected birds the day before, his wife said, from two neighbouring keepers. She couldn't tell me whether any of them had been melanistic.

To save time, I phoned those keepers. Neither had had a melanistic cock in the bag since late October.

'That's your starting-point,' I said. 'Mr Taylor's the head keeper at Boyes Castle. He'll be home by the time you can get there. He's a nice old chap and not a gossip. You want to know where a melanistic cock, this year's bird, was shot. It had been feeding on barley stubble and also turnip-seed and it had a dark red wing-tag with this year's date on it.'

Ian was looking unhappy. 'What's the significance of the wing-tag?' he asked.

I tried not to look impatient. Ian had been coming on well as a clay pigeon shot and I was inclined to forget that his new-found knowledge of the countryside and field sports was still largely superficial. 'Some keepers just put birds into the release pens and count how many are bagged in the season. Anything around a fifty per cent return is counted as pretty good. More conscientious keepers want to know how many of their own birds they're getting as opposed to inward migrants and wild stock, so they'll tag their birds with a different colour each year. The really good keepers, and I'd expect Mr Taylor to be among them, use different tags for different release pens so that they can tell, after the birds have been free for three months or more, which pen each one came from. That way, they can measure the success of each release area, how far the birds have wandered from it and so whether any pens need to be moved.'

'But they can wander a hell of a long way, can't they? I mean, they're birds.'

'They're birds,' I admitted, 'but they're not birds of passage. They're pedestrians, not aviators. If the cover's good and they have feed and water, they don't wander very far. Especially the cocks.'

Ian was still struggling to understand. 'I thought they'd wander off in search of the hens.'

'Other way round,' I told him. I nearly added that they were just like people but I decided to leave him with the illusion that man was still the hunter.

He scratched his neck, looking even less happy. 'I'll have to do this myself,' he said at last. 'I can't have the local bobby tramping around asking questions. But you'd better come with me. You know the language. Can you get away? Delia's life . . . '

'Yes, of course,' I said. 'Samantha can look after the office and Madge Foullis can oversee the factory. As soon as the prep-room's working again.'

He glared at me but he knew that I had him by what Dad would have called the short and curlies. 'If you're right about the beads, and if they were dropped where she was being taken, and if she's still there and if a dozen other things, we may be messing about within sight of whoever's holding her. I don't think they'll know me by sight but I don't want to start anyone thinking by circling around in a shiny car with two aerials. We need something that looks like part of the local scene. Any chance of borrowing your uncle's old Land Rover?'

'He's gone up north. Anyway, I wouldn't be seen dead in it. He's probably gralloched a deer in the back of it and not bothered to clean it out. I could probably borrow Dad's jeep if he's at the shop.'

'Phone him,' said my lord and master, 'while I get the contents of those birds' crops collected. Then let's go!'

Dad, who was again stuck with minding the shop and inclined to get peevish about it, said that I might as well have the jeep for all the good it was doing him, rusting away in the Square. If he didn't get it back by closing time Mum could damned well come and fetch him in the family hatchback and serve her right, because by rights she should have been in the shop but instead . . . And so on and so forth.

So Ian left his car at the police building behind the town hall and I drove the jeep. Almost as an afterthought I collected Sam. The old dog rather enjoyed spending most of the working days in the shop where he could greet old shooting friends with a sniff and a wag, but he appreciated an outing now and again. The back of the jeep was already full, but Sam was quite used to making himself a nest among Dad's pigeon decoys and camouflage nets.

We left the town, passed my old home and headed towards Edinburgh. As we laboured up Soutra Hill on to the top of the Lammermuirs, Ian roused himself from a reverie and said, 'It's a hell of a long shot.'

'Yes,' I said. There was no point denying it. 'If it doesn't come off, what'll you do?'

'Some of the big bugs want to haul in the directors of Sempylene and see what a mixture of bluff and veiled threats will achieve.'

We levelled out and picked up speed again. The rain was holding off but a cold breeze tried to push the top-heavy little vehicle off the road and into the heather. 'That could be fatal for Delia,' I said.

'That's what I've been telling them.'

'Well, tell them again from me.'

'Then both our heads could be on the block if they try it and it works. Anyway, if word's leaked out that Thrower's in our hands, she's probably dead by now.'

We crossed the Lammermuirs in silence and I turned off to the east.

'I didn't realise that Boyes Castle was over this way,' Ian said. 'It's off my patch.'

'Does that matter?'

'Not yet. What can you tell me about Mr Taylor and the place?'

The sun came out as we descended towards the coastal plain. I groped for Dad's sunglasses. 'I've known him for years,' I said. 'He used to be a beatkeeper near Newton Lauder. All through my teens I went beating for him and got invited to the Keeper's Day at the end of the season, when the beaters and pickers-up get to shoot and the syndicate members beat for them. I didn't see much of him after he moved to Boyes Castle as head keeper until he phoned Dad, nearly two years ago. He was in a pickle because the laird – Nigel Farquharson – had a Boxing Day shoot coming up and those of his beaters who weren't sick or in jail had had better offers to go and beat on one of the big commercial shoots.'

'Would that be the Farquharson who showed up at our wedding? The shipowner?'

'I suppose you could call him that, although I don't think that shipping's much of an earner these days. Dad and Ronnie postponed their own shoot, gathered up a few friends and went to help him out. Mr Taylor was so grateful, I think he'd have done a human sacrifice if Mr Farquharson had let him. And I still see him occasionally when it's his turn to bring birds to the factory.'

Ian was quiet. I glanced sideways and saw that he was looking uncertain.

'You know him well, then,' Ian said at last. 'Tell me this. Is he the sort of man who'd answer questions without asking why you wanted to know?'

I thought about Dod Taylor as I remembered him. 'Not if it concerned his birds,' I said.

'Could we cook up a good enough story to satisfy him?'

'I can't think of one, can you? He'd certainly remember whether his melanistic cock had been badly shot up. But he's a very upright sort of man. He doesn't drink or swear; and when he gossips it's polite gossip rather than malicious. Know what I mean?'

'Asking after relatives and mutual friends?'

'That sort of thing. I've never heard him say a spiteful word. I think he'd hold his tongue if you spelled it out and asked him to. Let me play it off the cuff.'

We were at the gates of Boyes Castle before Ian said, 'I can't think of a better approach. All right, we'll lay it on the line and trust him.'

'I think it's best,' I said.

On my previous visit, Dad had been driving and we had been heading for the rendezvous point rather than the head keeper's house, but some of the geography was coming back to me. The estate, which was parkland surrounded by a mixture of farmland and woods, seemed slightly unkempt, which was all to the good. Tidiness is the enemy of wildlife. The leaves, which were still hanging on in Newton Lauder and giving us a long autumn, were off the trees and blowing across the estate roads. After a few boss shots, which gave us occasional glimpses of the Victorian pseudo-castle built in the shape of an overgrown tower, I pulled off a road that ran between two woods of beech and drew up at Mr Taylor's door. Like many keepers' dwellings, his was a neat house with an immaculate front garden, backed by a shambles of sheds and enclosures.

Mrs Taylor came to the door. I had not seen her for years but I remembered her immediately – a talkative but motherly soul who had given me sweets and always made sure that my feet were dry when the day's beating was finished.

She had heard that I was now a married woman and she swept us inside and led the way slowly along a corridor, uttering exclamations of pleasure at meeting my new husband and enquiries after our enjoyment of the married state which ranged between the highly personal and the frankly ribald.

'Dod's just finishing his dinner,' she said. 'If you've been driving since you phoned, you'll not have eaten. There's no meat left, but there's soup and a bittie cheese and there's tea in the pot.' She opened the door on a bright kitchen. 'Dod, here's Miss Deborah come to see us and her new husband with her. Get up and tell her hello.'

Mr Taylor must have been nearing the age of retirement but he still looked very slim and fit. As a young man he would have been no Adonis, but the years in a life that he loved seemed to have toughened rather than aged him. His rather long nose was offset by kindly eyes, a ready smile and a general air of contentment. He got to his feet but his greeting had to wait while his wife bustled about, getting us seated and adding vegetables to plates of thick soup.

'I must away up to the big house,' she said at last. 'Mr Farquharson had visitors and I'm needed to lend a hand in clearing up after them. I'll leave you to chat in peace.'

Ian flicked a quick glance at me but I gave him a tiny headshake. She would be very unlikely to meet anyone other than the servants, but a warning to hold her tongue would only make her curious.

The room seemed very quiet after she had left it.

Although I had seen Mr Taylor at the factory for a few moments only the day before, he was meeting Ian for the first time. Custom required an exchange of news, comments on the weather and enquiries after friends. When the courtesies had been observed, he said, 'Well, now, Miss Deborah. You never came all this way just to make your new man known to us. What can I do for you?'

His shrewd eyes seemed to be looking right through me. No made-up story was going to satisfy him. It was a time for the truth. 'We've come to you for help,' I said. 'We may be on a wild-goose chase but, whether we're right or wrong, this is as confidential as anything ever can be.'

'Just ask,' he said. 'I'll not tell a soul. Not even Jeannie, if that's how it is.'

'Not even your pheasants,' I said. 'It's as secret as that. You read about the young girl who was kidnapped from Newton Lauder about ten days ago?'

'Aye.' His look of mild amusement vanished.

'She had a bracelet of glass beads of an unusual colour. Two beads that looked the same turned up in the crop of a pheasant. I think that it was among the ones you brought in to us yesterday.'

'There was a whole heap of birds from the Gorrington keeper with them,' Mr Taylor said. 'And some from Park House.'

'That brings us to the first question,' I said. 'It was a melanistic bird with a dark red wing-tag and this year's date. Was that yours or theirs?'

'Mine for sure. I'm using a new American tagger because there's a better range of colours. The Gorrington birds are all yellow-tagged this year. Park House don't tag, the lazy devil! The dark red tags were this year's releases in the Birken Wood pen. We've had three or four melanistics this year.'

'You wouldn't know where that one was shot?'

'At Red Burn,' he said promptly. 'There was only the yin

92

this time round. He'd stayed close to home. The beaters put him out of Birken Wood and Mr Henry Clevely pulled him down from quite forty yards up, a lovely shot. Och, but you maun be wrong.'

'But the bird was yours?' Ian said.

'Aye. That I must admit. But I canno' believe. No, no, lassie. The beads must have come here by some other way.'

'What other way?' I asked.

'In the grain that's in the feeders, maybe.'

'Barley?'

'Wheat,' he said.

'There was barley in the bird's crop.'

He frowned unhappily. 'I just . . . ' Then he stopped and snapped his fingers. 'There was gravel brought in just last week, to patch some of the tracks. The beads will have come in with it.'

'Where did the gravel come from?' Ian asked.

'You'd have to ask the laird about that.'

'Not just yet,' Ian said. 'How do we get to Red Burn?'

'When you've finished, I'll take you there. My under keeper's away on a course and I'll need to be topping up the feeder.' Mr Taylor spoke more easily, now that he was back on familiar ground. 'They're not taking much from it, there's that much feeding on the ground still, but it helps to keep them close and they'll know where to come when the hungry part of the year comes round again.'

Ian drained his mug of tea. 'Thank Mrs Taylor for the soup,' he said. 'We were needing it.'

We followed the keeper outside. I fetched Dad's binoculars from the jeep and we crammed ourselves into the front of Mr Taylor's pick-up.

He turned off the estate road to bounce along a track that was little more than a path beaten through long grass by occasional wheels and feet. Tools clattered in the back of the pick-up. Mallard took to the air as we skirted a small lake. We followed the feeder stream into a shallow valley. Ahead of us, pheasants scurried into the bushes. The track petered out in a small area of bare earth reinforced in places with fresh gravel. We got out of the pick-up.

Mr Taylor pulled two half-bags of grain to the tailgate of the pick-up and then paused. He nodded towards a nearby stake which bore a card with the number 3. 'Yon's where Mr Clevely stood,' he said. 'The melanistic cock took off from the top of the hill and he was still climbing.' I looked where Mr Taylor was pointing and developed a respect for Mr Clevely. The bird must have looked as small as a starling.

The keeper picked up both of the bags, one in each hand, but Ian took one from him and swung it over his shoulder. Mr Taylor nodded a thank you and set off at a smart pace along a path that climbed obliquely up the hill. Ian followed and I fell in behind him. When he began to flag, I gave him a helpful push. My muscles were probably more accustomed to carrying sacks of feed around than his were, but I decided to let him bear the burden. The exercise would do him good and I wanted him to realise that any heavy loads were his to carry.

The trees at the top were very open, with plenty of under-growth to provide shelter for the birds. At our arrival, pigeon clattered out of the branches overhead. The feeder stood in a clearing outside a now empty release pen, large enough to have held several hundred birds without any excuse for feather-pecking. Mr Taylor lifted the lid off the feeder.

'You're giving them wheat?' Ian asked.

'Aye. Still with some pellets.'

'Where's the nearest barley stubble?' I asked.

'The good Lord knows,' Mr Taylor said, still decanting grain into the feeder. I exchanged an anguished glance with Ian. Could we be so totally wrong? Could the beads have come in with the gravel after all? 'There was barley just over the hill,' the keeper added. 'The stubble was ploughed a fortnight back, but there'd be grain left along the hedge where the combine couldn't reach it.'

We breathed again.

Mr Taylor folded the empty bags carefully and then led the way towards the further edge of the trees. A windbreak hedge fringed the wood, but even so Ian drew us across to where a small clump of evergreens formed a ready-made screen. We peered out like some animal from its lair.

The ground fell away into flat farmland, a patchwork of grass and stubble and plough. A tractor was working in the distance, its noise brought faintly to us on the breeze. Below, another hedge ran away from us, separating a large pasture from an even larger field, recently ploughed. There were no sheep or cattle on the grass but I could make out one or two pheasants scratching for insects in the dung or picking clover.

Beyond a thin strip of pines which gave shelter from the north there was a house. The hedge formed one of the boundaries of a garden run riot. Through Dad's binoculars I thought that I could make out the dead stalks of turnips run to seed. The house, made small by distance, was partly screened by the treetops, but it seemed to be a substantial stone house, two rooms square and two storeys high with a roof of blue-black slates, set down uncompromisingly in the flat countryside. A drive followed the hedge to a road a hundred yards beyond.

The house seemed deserted, but through the binoculars I could detect a faint heat-shimmer over one chimney and a trace of smoke. Then I noticed a slightly open window. A small splodge of a different grey seemed to be a vehicle tucked close against the back of the house.

'Who owns the house?' Ian asked.

'Dashed if I know,' Mr Taylor said. 'I'd forgotten all about the place. An old couple lived in it, but she died at the turn of the year and he followed in the spring. It stood empty after that.'

'Are those turnip-heads in the back garden?' I asked.

'They could well be,' Mr Taylor said. 'It was this way. The old man was a bit of a tiger. About two years back, he chased some loons out of the garden where they'd been after apples. Gave them a clout or two with his stick, they say. Their parents wanted to make a case of it, but the local bobby said that they'd asked for it. The upshot was that they paid the old chap back by tossing some turnip-seed into his garden. Just terrible, the fertility of neip-seeds. They were coming up as weeds by the thousand and he never did get rid of them all.'

'The house is supposed to be empty?' I asked.

'I thought it was. I'm dashed if you mayn't be right after all. I hope so, for the wee lass's sake.'

'There's somebody there now.' Ian scratched his neck. He was thinking aloud. 'It's still a long shot, but we've got to assume that there may be men, probably armed, holding

96

a hostage. I'll have to call Edinburgh for assistance. May I use your phone?'

'Aye.'

'I don't want to use the radio more than I have to – if they're professionals, they'll be monitoring the police channels. Until back-up arrives, I'll have to keep watch.'

'From up here?' said Mr Taylor.

'It's not ideal. This is the back of the house. If they suddenly decided to leave by the front, we couldn't stop or follow them. But the other side's as bare as . . . '

I had been using the binoculars. 'Look beyond the house and beyond the road and slightly right,' I said. 'There's a low hump with gorse-bushes, beyond the rape stubble, and a track running up from the road.'

'We couldn't get there without being seen from the house,' Ian said. 'If we spook them now, we could put the girl's life in jeopardy.'

'Maybe,' I said. 'But not if there was an obvious and reasonable reason for our going there. Are those fields part of the estate?'

'They are,' said Mr Taylor. 'Not part of the shoot, though.'

'There are pigeon dropping in, just this side of the gorse,' I said.

Ian snatched the binoculars away from me and re-focused them. 'By God!' he said. 'You're right!'

Six

I checked the contents of Dad's jeep while Ian used Mr Taylor's phone. With Wallace nursemaiding Sir Peter, Dad had not been free to go after the pigeon for some weeks but he had lived in hope. The gear was all there, including the two guns which were almost a permanency in the locked compartment under the rear floor.

Ian came out at last, followed by Mr Tayor. 'My help's there if you want it,' the keeper said. 'I've no liking for men who carry off young girls.'

Ian paused in thought and then shook his head. 'Thanks,' he said. 'I may come back to you. For the moment, two of us at the front will be enough. Until back-up arrives, I'll be in radio touch with my local colleagues.'

'Good luck, then,' Mr Taylor said.

Ian dropped into the passenger seat and I drove back around the Boyes estate roads.

'It's going to take time to get the men here,' he said. 'If we're hasty, we'll turn a kidnapping into a hostage-holding.'

'Or even a murder,' I said.

'Right.'

I let the jeep slow to a halt. 'Maybe my idea was stupid. If you were holding a kidnap victim, wouldn't you be suspicious of a pair of pigeon-shooters setting up opposite your front door?'

'I've been wondering the same thing. On the whole, I think not. I'd take notice, but I wouldn't expect the police to think along those lines – especially not a man and a girl. We'll be about a quarter of a mile off and it seems to me that they must by now be fed up of going to red alert every time a man on a tractor starts working nearby. I think they'll accept us as part of the country scene.'

We moved off again. 'And if they don't?' I asked. We left the gates of the estate and made a turn which I guessed would bring us past the house.

'I've asked for two plain cars to be waiting, one near the nearest junction in each direction. If we think that Delia's being removed, we tip them off and they block the road. I fixed up some very short code-words, for whenever we have to break radio silence. That's the best we can do until reinforcements arrive. Or isn't it?' he added uncertainly. 'Have I missed anything?'

'Not a thing,' I said.

With unnerving suddenness the trees ended, the country-side opened up and we saw the house ahead, set well back from the road on the right-hand side. I kept my eyes strictly ahead while Ian leaned back and stole a glance behind the back of my neck.

'Looks quiet,' he said, 'but I think there was a face near one of the windows. Be natural. Don't even think about anything but the woodies. Go left here.'

I had already identified the mouth of the track. It was hardly more than a pair of wheel-ruts, made by tractors and awkwardly spaced for the narrow jeep. The rape stubble was on our left. On the other side, beyond a wire fence, was what looked like a harvested potato-field. A few greylag geese, grazing on the remains of the potatoes, ignored us but a cloud of pigeon went up from the rape and headed for the trees where we had been a half-hour earlier.

'I hope they come back,' I said as I pulled up beside the gorse-bushes. 'If they don't, we'll look daft staying more than twenty minutes or so.'

Ian grunted. 'Twenty minutes may be enough,' he said.

We dumped Sam and the gear out of the back of the jeep. True to form, Dad had a couple of hundred cartridges neatly stowed. By good luck, I was wearing a dress of suitably neutral colour and sensible shoes, but I had come away with only a thin coat. I appropriated Dad's waxproof coat and gave Ian the camouflaged shooting jacket to cover his white shirt. Then I drove the jeep on, turned in a gateway and came part of the way back. There was nowhere to hide the vehicle, so I left it far enough off to be ignored by the birds. Pigeon know the range of a shotgun very well but they are too accustomed to seeing vehicles in the fields to associate them with the probability of an ambush in the near distance.

Ian had already set up a camouflage net to screen off a space between two gorse-bushes and was setting out some plastic decoys. In his few years of associating with me and my family, he had been learning. The pattern of decoys looked very natural as they bobbed in the breeze. I let him finish while I pulled up some dead grass and weeds to dress the camouflage net.

Always the gentleman when reminded, Ian gave me the use of Dad's fishing-stool and settled himself uncomfortably on a small rock from where he could bring the binoculars to bear on the house through the base of one of the

gorse-bushes. I glanced once and once only in the same
direction. The house stood out clearly, but in the damp
air the trees on the higher ground beyond were no more
than a fuzz. Sam curled down beside my feet. After a few
moments Ian dropped the binoculars down the inside of his
jacket, put his radio carefully to hand and took up Dad's
oldest twelve-bore.

'Did you see anything?' I asked.

'Not a damn thing. Mr Taylor may be right. Perhaps
those beads came in with the gravel. But I felt watched.
You do most of the shooting while I keep observation.'

'Shouldn't you get somebody to speak to Mr Farquharson
and find out where the gravel came from?' I asked.

'Not yet.'

'Why not?'

'The time isn't ripe,' he said shortly.

After five minutes, the birds had begun to forget that we
were there. A single pigeon flew over. We left him alone.
Pigeon behaviour and tactics are the subject of endless
argument, but I had come to agree with Dad that these
scouting singletons should be spared. Let the flight-line
develop and it will continue under its own momentum.

A trickle of birds began, in twos and threes, coming in
high over the field and then homing in on the decoys. I
missed the first and then began to score. My third kill
landed on its back, a danger-signal to approaching birds.
I would have gone out to set up the dead birds as extra
decoys but after Ian's words I knew that I would have had
stage-fright. I lifted the corner of the net and sent Sam, who
knew exactly what was wanted of him. In his old age, he
ambled out into the field instead of racing over the stubble
as he would have done in his youth. He ignored the decoys

and the tidily dead and brought the inverted bird back to hand, settling down at my feet again with a contented grunt and glancing up for approval. I scratched his head, telling him that life was not over yet.

'That should present them with a suitably uncoplike image,' Ian said.

The radio woke up suddenly. 'Come in, Harry,' it said. The words were repeated several times.

'Harry's the code for the car at the junction near the Boyes Castle gates,' Ian said. 'They're telling me that it's in place. That was quick.'

'If that was quick,' I said, 'I don't know that we can wait for slow.'

'These things take time,' Ian said. 'They must have had a car nearby. Now they'll be rearranging schedules, bringing cars in from further afield and asking each other whether I know what the hell I'm doing. I'm beginning to wonder the same thing.'

'In about an hour,' I said, 'if their little crops are full, the pigeon are going to go for a drink and then up to roost and the supply will dry up. Only a prat or a policeman would hang on after that. A real shooting person would move to the woods.'

'I don't suppose that these are real shooting persons,' Ian said anxiously. 'They're city boys.'

'I hope to God they're as ignorant as you think they are.'

'Don't sow these doubts in my mind,' he said. 'One of my bosses may be coming out to take over, but for the moment it's my baby.'

It came to me that his new responsibilities were weighing on him. Until a few months earlier, he had been the sergeant who carried out orders from on high. 'You're doing everything possible,' I said. 'If they find her here, the credit will go to you.'

I brought down another five birds and Ian two. One of his was only winged, a runner. Old Sam showed that he still had a spurt or two left in him.

The shadows were beginning to stretch out and our visitors were becoming fewer. Ian began to fidget. 'The other car should have been in position by now,' he said. 'And somebody was to go to Mr Taylor's house and be guided up to where we were this morning. Where the hell is everybody? All we need,' he said disgustedly, 'is a sudden riot in Edinburgh and nobody having time for me and my trivial problems any more.'

After a few more minutes the radio suddenly woke up again. 'Come in, Deborah,' it said. 'Harry calling.'

Ian grabbed it. 'I think it's for me,' I said.

He shook his head. 'Yours was one of the few names I could think of in a hurry. They're telling me that they have a message for me.'

'It's about time we packed up,' I said.

Ian frowned in concentration. A late pigeon swept in low and landed among the decoys before I was ready for him.

'Could you hang on here for a minute?' Ian asked suddenly.

'A minute, yes,' I said. 'An hour, forget it!'

'You wouldn't be scared? I could walk there and back. For all the men in the house would know, I could be going to another car for a flask or some more cartridges. I don't want to leave the house unwatched. I'll leave you my radio. If I give the word . . . Think of a name.'

103

'Ian,' I said. The pigeon either heard my voice or was spooked by the immobility of its companions. It took off. I missed behind.

Ian looked at me expectantly and then grasped my meaning. 'That'll do. If you hear "Come in, Ian" on the radio, pack up and join me at the gates of Boyes Castle. If anything moves, press the "Transmit" button three times. But if a vehicle leaves and turns right from the house – their right, not yours – press it and keep on pressing it over and over again. We'll hear it clicking and we'll come after them. If they leave and turn left, press "Transmit" and tell me and we'll follow them up.'

'I can do that,' I said. 'But don't forget that they may be armed.'

'I won't forget,' he said. 'By God I won't.'

'Well, don't. You stay out of the rough stuff and I'll do the same.'

He gave me his best, number one grin. 'Good girl. And if anybody leaves the house and seems to be heading in your direction, leave everything, get in the jeep and go. Across country, if you have to.'

'Don't think I wouldn't.'

He looked at me doubtfully for a moment but my words seemed to reassure him. He gave me a quick peck on the side of the nose, stepped out of the hide and set off across the rape stubble, slanting across to hit the road at the far corner beyond the house. He was carrying Dad's gun over his arm. I nearly called him back and took it off him, because a man with a gun is much more likely to have a rush of courage to the head than one without, but decided to let him keep it. Dad believes that people should be allowed to defend themselves; and I have never seen why that privilege should not be extended to policemen.

It seemed that my function was to keep watch. I tried to observe without turning my head. The house just sat there, impassive and bland. Even the smoke at the chimney had died or was being swept away by a rising breeze. Ian reached the road and went out of my sight.

I was suddenly very much alone in an empty landscape. Courage drained away, leaving a vacant place in the pit of my stomach. The cold wind seemed to cut through me.

A small flock of pigeon swept over while I was watching the house. To have ignored them would have been to signal that I was not a *bone fide* shooter. I was just in time to knock one down and miss another. And then, just as I had predicted, the visitations dried up.

How long, I wondered, would Ian expect me to wait? How long before the enemy became suspicious of a lonely girl watching decoys while the birds were streaming to roost?

I turned my attention back to the house and was just in time for a glimpse of a figure disappearing round the corner. I decided to let Ian know that the occupants were stirring.

Pressing the Transmit button produced sundry clicks and hisses, so I was satisfied that something was happening. All the same, when my husband's voice suddenly said, 'Come in, Ian,' I was so startled that I almost dropped the radio.

I was free to move at last and suddenly I wanted to be a long way away, in front of a fire with a large gin and nothing in one hand and Ian in the other. I fetched the jeep first, just in case, and left its engine running, ready for a quick departure. Packing up a pigeon layout can be a slow business, but I bundled everything higgledy-piggledy into the back of the jeep; dead birds, decoys, cartridges, gun and camouflage nets all mixed together, with Sam sprawled across the top. Dad wouldn't be pleased, but to hell with him! He wasn't alone in hostile territory with night approaching.

The jeep bounced and tried to take over its own steering as I drove, too fast, down the track. At the road, I had to wait for a moment as a tractor went slowly by, pulling a trailerload of straw bales. I sighed with impatience, but in a moment I would be accelerating away up the road out of harm's way. The tractor went clear.

The jeep's engine was limping. It must have been cold. I coaxed the jeep out into the road and once we were moving I trod hard on the accelerator.

That proved to be a mistake. The engine picked up, hesitated, chuffed a couple of times and then died on me. I declutched quickly in the hope that I could roll out of sight, but there was no slope to help me along. I coasted a few yards past the driveway of the house before I ran out of momentum and came to a gentle halt.

When Dad taught me to drive, he also gave me a short course on what happens under the bonnet. Except around guns I might not be much of a mechanic, but at least I was not entirely clueless as to how the thing worked. Or didn't. My best guess was a fuel problem. In the hope that the trouble was no more than an airlock I got out of the vehicle and blew down the petrol-filler a few times. Then I hopped back into the driving-seat and tried the starter. The engine coughed twice and died again.

'Stay calm and think,' I told myself. In hindsight, I now

106

know that was the worst advice I ever received, from myself or anyone else. It would have been the right time to panic, to do exactly what I most wanted to do – to leap from the vehicle and run screaming up the road. But one never knows these things at the time.

So I stayed calm and thought. And almost immediately, I saw the answer staring me in the face. Unlike any other car I had ever driven, Dad's jeep had a manual choke. The choke control was still protruding, taunting me. I had flooded the damned thing.

I had made the same mistake once before and I could still hear Dad's voice. 'Choke in, foot hard down on the accelerator and give it a long spin. If that doesn't do it, go for a long walk while the plugs dry.' The long walk sounded the more attractive, but I tried the first part of the advice. From the noises under the bonnet, the battery was going to fail before the engine fired.

I said a word that Dad had used when somebody backed a Land Rover over his favourite gun. I still don't know what it means, but it relieved my feeling a little.

Ian's radio was buried somewhere in the jumble in the back. He would not want me to leave it where somebody could find it and listen in or even send bogus messages; and if I had it in my hand I could scream for help if somebody grabbed me. I knelt on the seat and groped among the camouflage nets and dead birds, pushing aside the heavy and now somnolent Sam.

The radio eluded me but after several frantic minutes my fingers touched the muzzles of the gun. That, I decided, would do just as well. I could not quite reach to grasp it. The driver's door was open behind me. As I stretched further, somebody goosed me. I would have suspected

Sam, whose cold nose has been known to catch ladies in short skirts unaware, but Sam was in front of me and snoring again.

My nerves were already stretched. The sudden evidence that I was no longer alone was almost too much. I executed several simultaneous manoeuvres, none of them voluntary. I gave a leap that hit my head against the jeep's roof, uttered a loud squawk, swallowed back some vital organ which had tried to jump out of my mouth and spun round, banging my hip on the steering wheel. Behind me, Sam grunted, decided that this was not the time for play and began snoring again.

A man grabbed my elbow and pulled me out onto the road.

'You keep your hands to yourself,' I said. For the moment, indignation had taken over from fear.

'If you leave a bum like that sticking up in the air,' he said, 'you must expect it to be grabbed. We were waiting our chance to move, and now you can come along for the ride. Don't try to scream or I'll belt you one.'

I believed him. He was burly, with a strongly featured face. The cast of his features combined toughness with a sort of humour, like a playful bulldog. His was the type that goes zestfully into any wickedness. He would fight fiercely over little or nothing and then share a drink and a laugh with his opponent while they compared the damage. I might not have recognised the type if my Uncle Ronnie had not been cast in the same mould.

A battered Transit van had come down the drive from the house and was halting at the gate. The back doors opened. He pulled me across and pushed me inside and down to the floor, climbing in after me. The van moved off.

Two other people were in the back of the van. As I was pushed inside I had a photographic glimpse of a thin man with hot eyes, perched on one of the bench seats that ran down either side. Mrs Thrower's brief description had been remarkably acute. And sharing the bare floor with me, crouching almost nose to nose, was Delia, still in her school uniform. Her hair was untidy and her clothes seemed to be overdue for the laundry although she herself looked undamaged. There was even a smell of soap clinging to her. But her face was tear-stained and she was sucking her thumb.

'Are you all right?' I asked her.

She took her thumb out of her mouth but no answer followed it. I could see her problem. How all right was 'All right'? I tried to rephrase the question and ran into a difficulty of my own. I was not sure whether she would understand the terms, or even the concept, of sexual interference. Nor was I quite sure that I wanted to know.

'Have they bad used you?' I asked.

She hesitated again and then shook her head, but her eyes brimmed over.

'No talking,' said the man who had grabbed me. 'And don't look up. Neither of you's too old for a good spanking.' He sounded more amused at the idea than I felt.

'Let 'em talk if they want to,' the thin man said in a flat, metallic voice. 'I'd rather have talk than the eternal snivelling.'

After that, of course, there seemed to be nothing comforting to say that would not have meant more to our captors than to Delia.

It was one of Dad's guiding principles that as long as

there was something you could usefully do you kept your head and did it. 'After that,' he told me, 'you can have hysterics if you want to.' (I really must stop quoting Dad and invent a few aphorisms of my own.) I might have welcomed a refreshing attack of hysteria, but somebody had to keep their head and it seemed unlikely that that person would be Delia. She had resumed her thumb-sucking. I tried to apply reason to the available facts.

The van had turned away from the castle gates. If an observer had already arrived at the release pen he would have seen our departure and the alarm would have been raised. And perhaps the other police car was even now in place. But we had only driven for a minute or so when we turned off again onto a rougher surface.

'Nothing yet,' said the voice of the thinner man. I cocked an eye up and sideways and saw that he was nursing a transistor radio. Ian had been right. They were monitoring the police frequencies. If no more messages had been passed, then it seemed to follow that only the one car was in place.

We had turned off the road in the direction of the castle. So we must have been on one of the estate roads. Were they using a short cut through the estate to bypass a roadblock? Or were we heading for the castle itself? If Mr Farquharson was not in residence, it was possible that they had the use of some building from whomever had let them into the house. On the other hand, I remembered that guests had only recently left the castle. And Ian had been doubtful about telling the whole story to Mr Taylor. Logic led me onward.

I tried looking at it from a different viewpoint. The police had been searching for one or more confederates who had been Sir Humphrey Peace's secret partner in what I thought was called 'insider trading'. But the two had not met until my wedding. I had introduced them.

That little scene was clear in my mind. They had certainly denied knowing each other. Mr Farquharson had taken the supercilious line that he usually reserved for his social inferiors. 'I think that you once shot a friend of mine . . .' Despite all the distractions of the wedding reception I had been surprised. Even if true, it was not the sort of thing that one landowner says to another on first acquaintance. The words were the deadliest insult. Yet Sir Humphrey Peace, a fastidiously careful man, had seemed amused. At the time, I put it down to consideration for my feelings. In retrospect, it seemed more like genuine amusement at a clever way of ramming home the message that the two had never previously met.

If Nigel Farquharson had been a major purchaser of shares during the run-up to the takeover, the finger of suspicion might already have been pointed in his direction if not actually inserted into a sensitive part of his anatomy. Much would depend on whether any point of contact between the two men had been uncovered. But no. If Mr Farquharson had already been a prime suspect, observation would surely have been kept on the castle and its vicinity. The presence of potential kidnappers would hardly have gone unnoticed.

Next question – had Mr Taylor betrayed us to his boss? On the whole, I thought not. But Mrs Taylor had been on her way up to the castle. Did she know that I had married a policeman? Probably. It had been in the local papers. An innocent mention of a visit from Miss Deborah and her policeman husband might have set alarm bells ringing.

Delia was grizzling quietly. I patted her hand and tried to ignore her.

What would Ian do when he found the deserted jeep? Without knowing how complete was the net which he had been drawing around the house, it was impossible to guess. Would he think that we had been whisked out of the area and waste his energies sending messages far and wide? That might depend on the route and timing of the second roadblock car. I realised suddenly that Sam was still in the jeep. Would Sam be able to follow the van up by scent? I thought not. He had a good nose but he was no bloodhound.

I had no time for any more ineffectual pondering. The van crunched on to gravel, swung round a last curve and reversed abruptly. The thickset man opened the van's back doors and both men jumped down. The driver had never even turned his head.

'Out you come.'

The van had been backed up to the open doorway of what seemed to be an empty lock-up garage. I followed the men out and helped Delia down.

'You can't just shut us in here like animals,' I said.

But it seemed that they could. The van pulled forward the length of one long stride and the up-and-over garage door was pulled down, slammed and locked. I had no more than a glimpse of the outside world but I had seen the skyline and recognised the towering shape of Boyes Castle.

As soon as the door was down, Delia gave way to her tears. At the same time, she started an outpouring of incoherent questions. Those that I could distinguish between her sobs were much the questions I had been asking myself.

Why had we been moved? Did anybody know that we were here? What was going to happen to us?

I gave her the comfort of a hug. She seemed to expect to be nursed but, remembering Dad's advice, I decided against wasting time in useless chatter.

'Be brave,' I said firmly but without much hope. 'Be a big girl, the way your Daddy would want.'

To my surprise, the weeping stopped. 'When are we going home?' she asked.

'I don't know,' I said. 'Keep your voice down. They may have left somebody on guard. We've got to get out of here.'

The thought of escape seemed to be new to her. 'But why?' she whispered. 'We're hostages, aren't we? They've been telling me that I'd have nothing to worry about as long as Daddy did nothing to spoil things for them.'

I could have pointed out that the prospects of hostages, who were also witnesses, were less than good once their usefulness was over, but that might have pushed her over the edge. 'We don't know what's going to happen,' I said, 'and we'd be better out of the way. We don't want to be hostages when the police start closing in. That might make it difficult for them to rescue us.' I bit off the word 'alive' before it could slip out.

'If that's what you think,' she said doubtfully.

'Of course it's what I think. Do you want a pistol at your head when they come?'

I had been looking around our prison by what little light came in through a small, barred window that faced onto a blank wall about a foot away. There was a light fitting on the ceiling but the conduit for its wiring disappeared through the angle of roof and wall, evidently to a switch outside.

Every similar garage that I had ever seen had been like Ian's, containing many years' accumulation of discarded items that might be wanted again some day, but this one had been cleared and swept clean.

'Look around,' I said. 'Or if it's too dark, feel. See if you can find anything we could use as a tool. Anything at all. And be quick. The light will be gone soon.'

'All right.'

The nuts and bolts joining the concrete units seemed to be rusted together. Unless Delia found a discarded spanner, our chance of dismantling the garage from within were negligible. Even without the bars, the window seemed impossible as an escape route. The garage itself was built of concrete units bolted together and the door was of sheet steel.

'Aren't you going to look?' Delia asked me.

'I'm looking for something different,' I said. 'Somewhere there has to be a weakest point. It may not be very weak, but wherever it is, we'll try there. You're smaller than I am. If we got the window out, could you squeeze through between the garage and the wall?'

She examined the window and then put her face against the glass to study the space outside. 'I'd get stuck,' she said.

The door seemed to offer us our only chance. It was strong, but it had been designed to be secure from the outside, not from within.

I felt in the pockets of Dad's coat, in the faint hope of finding a screwdriver or a pair of pliers; but they were empty except for a handkerchief.

I explored more by touch than by sight. The bolts holding the lock to the door were too tight for my fingers to turn. On the interior side of the lock a bar formed a double lever which pushed a pair of solid metal bars outwards to engage with the doorposts. If the bars would bend, they might disengage. I tried with all my might. They wouldn't.

Daylight was fading but the sun must have broken through for one last look at the land. There was a brightness on the wall facing the small window. It only lasted for a few seconds and then it was gone, but by its light I had seen what I had nearly missed – the weakest point. The bars fitted over pins on the lock-lever and were retained there only by split-pins and washers.

My fingers were already bruised and sore from my futile efforts to remove nuts from rusty bolts, but I sacrificed some more skin on those split-pins. Pain isn't there if you don't think about it, I told myself, but I knew that I was lying. The pins were thick and they resisted every effort to straighten them enough to withdraw from their holes. With the proper tools – pliers, a knife, even a nail file – it would have been the work of a second or two. Without them it was impossible.

Delia was tapping my arm. 'This is all I could find,' she said. The place had looked so bare that I had set her to searching the corners mostly to keep her out of my hair. I nearly waved her away. But when I looked down, she was offering me an old and rusted washer, a thing of no account, discarded, long past its useful life – except that it was the very thing I needed.

The bent ends of the split-pins kept turning away from my pressure but I perservered, trying at the same time to work in silence in case there was a guard outside the door or one of the men chose the wrong moment to pass by. When I had the split-pins as straight as I could get them, they still refused to come out through their holes.

It took me five minutes of pushing with the washer and wiggling and sheer bloody-minded willpower to get one of those damned pins out. I was just about to begin work on the other when I heard several sets of footsteps approaching. I tried to put the split-pin back, but of course the ends had sprung apart again and refused to enter. A key scratched in the lock. I left the pin hanging in the mouth of the hole and jumped back. The light overhead came on and the door went up and slid back above our heads.

We blinked in the sudden brilliance. When my eyes recovered, I saw that four men stood ranked across the doorway, studying us dispassionately. As the door went up they moved forward and we retreated. Delia moved closer and took my hand. We gripped. For once, I was glad of the contact.

I had only set eyes on Nigel Farquharson, the laird of Boyes Castle, three or four times before, and one of those times had been at my wedding when, in proper morning suit, he had seemed arrogant but harmless. Now, with the big-bellied figure enlarged by thick tweeds and the eyes, half buried in the puffed flesh, further hidden under the shadow of a tweed hat from which his hooked nose protruded like a predatory beak, he was a figure from a monster video. He looked at me hard and then spoke to the man on his right, whose face I had never seen before. From the shape of his ears I guessed that he had been the driver of the van. He looked ordinary enough to have been Elaine Anderton's assailant.

'You were right,' Farquharson said. 'That's the Calder

girl. She married a policeman and she'd hardly be shooting with some other man. They were keeping watch.' His accent was faintly American and I remembered somebody saying that he had spent years in the States.

The split-pin fell out of the door and tinkled on the floor behind him. The noise sounded like the clang of a gong to me, but nobody else noticed it.

On Farquharson's other side was the man who had snatched me out of the jeep. 'Ask her how they got on to us,' he said.

'That hardly matters now.'

'So what do we do?'

Farquharson shrugged. 'The jig's up. I guess it's always been up, ever since that damn-fool accountant chose the wrong moment to get horny. Well, the money's in Barbados and I'd rather roam the world rich than stay here trying to keep up style in a mouldering great house with about twopence a year coming in.' He raised his eyes in disgust. 'How would you like to buy a dozen ships off me cheap, all old and every damned one of them laid up, rusting away and costing the earth in mooring fees?'

'How much?' I said, in the hope of pulling his eyes down from the overhead door. The washer had dropped onto the brim of his tweed hat.

He looked at me with dislike but otherwise ignored me. 'And the sugar's gone out of farming,' he said. 'We've got an hour or two in hand. He wouldn't have had his wife with him if he'd been sure of his facts. He was just sniffing around but he found the scent he was looking for. The police are spread thin in country districts and it takes time to set up a cordon and get a search-warrant. After that, it'll be against their instincts to rush up to a castle and kick the door in. They'll come to the front door and knock.'

'So what do we do?' my captor asked again.

Farquharson looked at his watch. 'We don't get into a shooting war with the police. It'll be dark within the hour and the moon will come up soon after. Then we'll go. He'll have roadblocks at the junctions by then, but there are two Land Rovers in the bigger garage and we can go out across the fields. The *Venturer*'s still on charter to me and she's lying at Dunbar. I'll pay you the rest of your money there.'

The thin man said, 'What about these tarts?'

I felt Delia jump and I gave her hand an extra squeeze, hoping that she would take it as a signal to keep silent. Nothing that either of us could say would change his answer and Nigel Farquharson had been talking so freely that it was clear he had no intention of ever letting us go. But the bar which was now above his head had slipped. It was almost off the pin. If only they would finish and go, leaving us in the garage for a little longer . . .

'They come with us as far as Dunbar,' the big man said. 'We may have need of hostages again; and what better hostage than a copper's wife? After that . . . '

'We could dispose of them for you,' said the man with hot eyes. His tone did not suggest anything quick and merciful. For the first time I felt a shiver of something beyond fear, crawling sluglike up my backbone to leave a trail of slime on my mind.

'For a fee,' the driver added quickly.

The man with hot eyes hesitated and then nodded. However much he might enjoy his work, it was against his principles to work for nothing.

'After I've paid you what you're due,' Farquharson said slowly, 'I'll have very little sterling left—'

He had their full attention. They had even closed in on him, leaving a gap at the side of the doorway. Delia suddenly let go of my hand and shot through the gap. With a shout, the thin man took off after her.

I had already discounted the idea of trying to escape by means of sheer speed. The dusk was not yet deep enough to give us quick cover and, as Ian said once, 'If the average man couldn't run faster than the average woman, the human race would have died out long ago.' But Ian was only talking averages and Delia seemed to be going like a greyhound. It seemed only fair to gain her a sporting chance by causing a distraction. I dived for the now wider gap and the dusk beyond.

I nearly made it, but my earlier captor shot out an arm and caught the hood of Dad's coat. He swung me round, smiled pleasantly into my eyes and then gave me a slap on the side of my face that sent me spinning back into the garage and against the wall. I slid down into a crouching position and lowered my ringing head onto my arms. There was no room for thought in my head, the space was too taken up with shock and pain; but after some seconds I found the courage to touch my face with my fingertips. A swelling was already evident, but I thought that my cheekbone was not after all broken. If a few teeth were loose, no doubt the dentist could put me back together again. I had got off lightly.

As if from a great distance, I heard the thin man returning. Delia's feet dragged on the gravel behind him and then I heard her stumble as she was pushed inside. She came straight to me and put her arms around me. I let her comfort me while I wondered whether she had blown our last chance.

'I was about to say that I could dispose of them myself,' Farquharson said. 'Nothing easier, from a yacht. But there's a paid crewman aboard and I don't know what his reaction would be. So here's a proposition. I can't take the two Land Rovers with me. Neither of them's more than three years old. Keep them both for a fee. How's that?'

'Sounds good to me,' said the driver. 'I know a man who sends them abroad. The Arabs pay good money and no questions asked.'

'That's settled then,' Farquharson said. 'There are still some valuables in the house. Help me into the Land Rovers with them. Then we'll torch the place before we leave. That should keep the constabulary hands full, looking for hostages to rescue.'

'Jeepers!' said one of the men.

'Why not?' Farquharson said carelessly. 'I never liked the place. Now it's full of dry rot and woodworm and mortgaged three times over and it would take a Carnegie to keep it even halfway warm. Best use for it. Come along.'

Not one word had been addressed to us. We were no longer people.

I heard the door start to go down. I opened my eyes. They refused to focus together, but I was sure that the bar was slipping off its pin. I pulled myself loose from Delia's clutch and, scuttling forward on hands and knees, got a hand under it before it could clatter on the concrete, just as the door finished its descent. The light went out and suddenly the darkness was almost total. Footsteps receded, hurrying. The sun had gone down while they discussed our disposal.

I stayed where I was and covered my face. The sudden movement had set my head ringing again and I thought that I was probably going to throw up.

Delia put a hand on my shoulder. 'Don't cry,' she said. 'Please don't cry.'

'I'm not crying,' I said huskily. 'Really I'm not. Or if I am, it's more anger than hurt.' I gave myself a small shake and my head didn't quite fall off. 'Now you see why we've got to get out of here,' I told her. 'If we hold ourselves together, we'll be all right. Can you do that?'

'I'll try.' She was about to cork herself again with her thumb but she jerked her hand away.

I went back to work on the other split-pin, working by touch and memory. At least the task kept my mind off my other troubles. Suddenly the pin came free. I pulled both the steel bars right out of their sockets. They were heavy but manageable. I gave one to Delia.

'You carry this,' I said.

'Why?'

'If somebody tries to grab you again, swat him. Not just a prod but a good hard whack.' I looked her over. My one working eye was recovering after the brightness. Her school uniform was a grey skirt and blouse and a navy blazer, none of which would show up in the twilight. In the dim light, I could only make out her face and hands and, less clearly, her hair. 'When we go,' I said, 'move slowly. It's movement that catches the eye. Above all, don't turn your head for a look. Stick close to me unless we're seen. If we are, then run like hell.'

Then there was nothing to do but wait for the light to die. I thought of telling her about her father's crash, but decided not to add to her burdens.

Dusk comes slowly in northern latitudes but we needed the cover of near darkness. The timing was delicate. Delay might bring rescue; or it might bring Farquharson and his hired help with the Land Rovers. My only comfort was that Nigel Farquharson intended to wait for the rising of the moon. I hoped that he had his timings right, but I thought that a yachtsman ought to know things like the times of sunset and moonrise.

Somewhere nearby, I heard the mutter of a motorcycle engine and I remembered the bike that had nearly rammed me near Briesland House. The sound died and there was silence again.

After about twenty minutes, I decided to move. There was still a dull grey light outside. It might be too soon, but if we waited our chance might be gone. I lay down flat on the floor and pushed the bottom of the door out, very slowly, until I could make out, faint in the gloom, an empty yard, some black trees and a corner of the house.

I beckoned to Delia. She must have seen me because she crawled out after me and I pushed the door back into place.

We rose to our feet, each carrying one of the steel bars. To our right, I remembered from my brief moment of flight, the yard seemed to be enclosed by buildings. I moved forward. There was light diffused beyond the corner of the house and we had only taken a few steps before I saw the tailgate of a Land Rover. That way lay disaster. I turned left, towards a shrubbery backed with trees. A high wall extended from the garage, evidently a walled garden. The shrubbery it would have to be.

We slipped between two rhododendrons. The leaves rattled and Delia, following me, seemed to be breathing like an asthmatic but the men at the Land Rovers would have the sound of their own work and breathing in their ears. Daylight was further gone than I had thought but our time in the dark garage had brought us our night vision. I could make out a sort of pathway, probably the result of pruning forays by a gardener, and we moved along it, crouching.

After fifty yards, and at about the same distance from the lights around the castle door, the shrubbery finished at a great spread of lawns. I turned away, towards the trees, and came up against a wire fence. The top strand was barbed and when I touched one of the lower wires it squeaked like a wounded rabbit.

Seven

We squatted behind what I think, from the scent, must have been a mock orange and I took another look around while I thought.Neither process was easy. My left eye was almost closed and, on top of a pounding headache, I found that the blow had done something to my neck. Turning my head one way sent pain shooting up the long neck-muscle while any attempt to turn it in the other direction came up against a physical barrier.

All too near, almost within shotgun range, the Land Rovers stood in a pool of light. Figures moved around them and in and out of the big door but, rather than spoil my night vision, I tried not to look at them.

We had to move, and move soon. When we were missed, it would take only seconds to reason that there was only one direction in which we could have gone. There were dark clouds around the horizon but the sky was clear overhead. A moon that rose after dusk must be opposite the sun and therefore full. We had better get well away from the house before it turned the night into a pale imitation of day.

Should we risk the noise of the fence or the open of the grass? The breeze had dropped and the night was very quiet. Daylight was reduced to a lingering trace in the western sky and a slight softening of the darkness around us. I decided that the men were going in and out of lit rooms and their eyes would be night-blind. They would hear more than they would see. Only the backs of Delia's knees would shine – and her hair. I pulled her towards me and whispered to take her blazer off and wear it as a hood. She managed clumsily, still hugging the steel bar to her chest.

'I'm cold,' she said softly.

'Never mind,' I told her. 'You'll soon be warm now.' I meant that we would almost certainly have to run for it, but if she took comfort from thinking that I was promising her a hot bath and a cosy bed, so be it.

We walked softly, following the line of the fence away from the house so as to get as far as possible before we lost the screening of the shrubbery. We had made a hundred yards or more before there was a change to the light spilling from the house. My shadow was joined by its twin. There was a shout. The words were unclear but the meaning was obvious. Our absence was discovered.

The relief of precarious freedom turned into the terror of the hunted, but at least we were free to run. The time for pussyfooting was over. 'Come on,' I said. And we took to our heels, crossing the last of the grass towards the trees beyond. We made very little sound on the turf.

Would they waste precious time in coming after us? As we ran, I forgot my pains. I was pleased to discover that my mind was still functioning even if I did not like the answers it was giving me. There would certainly be pursuit. We had only to make contact with the outside world and mention Dunbar for Mr Farquharson to be up the proverbial creek without the *Venturer* to sail him out of it.

We reached the trees. Delia was ahead of me. She had lost her blazer along the way. Either she was very fleet of foot or her fear was even greater than mine. I cannoned into her in the darkness, catching my knee a crack against the steel bar that she was still hugging to her, and paused to recover my breath. I turned my head incautiously to snatch a look backward. There was a sharp click and the pain in my neck began to subside into an ache. Already there was a torch flickering in the shrubbery and voices were calling to each other. I heard the motorcycle engine splutter into life.

We plunged on, stumbling through low undergrowth in near-darkness. Brambles clutched at us, tearing skin and nylon. Pigeon, disturbed in their roost, rattled out of the branches overhead. The men would only have to stand still and listen and the birds would get their revenge for the afternoon's shooting by betraying us.

We were leaving the castle gardens for the less cultivated part of the estate which, further out, interwove with farmland. There was an open space in front of us and then more trees. The motorbike was moving fast, somewhere to our right. For the moment, we were still clear of our pursuers. The trees ahead had a blackness suggesting a more substantial woodland.

'Come on.' We said it together.

Just as we darted forward to cross the open, a flood of light grew around us. We stopped on the brink. Nigel Farquharson had got his sums wrong. The moon was already up but it had been behind the dark clouds to the east.

I hurled hate at the moon before I saw that it had saved us from running headlong into water. It was not, unfortunately, the flight pond that we had passed on our way to Birken Wood, which would have meant that we were back within a few hundred yards of where there would surely be police activity. This was larger, an acre of water among the woods.

Immediately, I could have pinpointed our position on an estate map. I remembered the lake from my previous visit. The road where I had left Dad's jeep was a long way off, somewhere to my right. Would help be waiting there? Probably, but not for sure. Mr Taylor's house was a little nearer, to the left. It came to me that he must be as ignorant of the kidnapping as he had seemed. If he had been one of the enemy he could have led us to some other release pen and we would never have known that we were being misled.

It was against my instincts to turn away from where Ian might be waiting, but enough time had elapsed for the police to have removed the jeep and themselves; and the sound of the motorbike had died away in that direction. The biker was searching there, or was lying in ambush in some strategic position.

We turned and ran to the left, along a rough path that I remembered. The guns had been placed at intervals along it and we beaters had come down the slope from the further side through a thick plantation of spruce. The going had been hard, even downhill, and I had ended up with scratchy needles down the back of my neck.

Thinking of the jeep had reminded me of poor Sam. If Ian was anywhere around, Sam would be with him. If, on the other hand, my husband had given me up, I hoped to live to have words with him.

I have few natural talents but one that I do have is unusual. Curling my tongue into a seemingly impossible shape, I can whistle loudly at a pitch at the very limit of human hearing. Dogs and children can hear it; women occasionally; men, especially those whose hearing has been damaged by shooting, almost never. It was a risk, but weighed against the chance of conveying a message through Sam it seemed worthwhile. I slowed, gathered my breath, rolled up my tongue and whistled with all my might. To me, it seemed deafening. Delia squeaked in protest and from the water a paddling of duck took fright and wing, but there was a good chance that nobody else had heard it.

The moon went in again behind a stray remnant of cloud. It was pitch-dark at ground level now and I had to lead the way almost by memory, gripping Delia's spare hand with mine. The lake showed clearly, reflecting the light of the stars, and an outline of the trees overhead helped me to keep my bearings. We had cleared the end of the lake when we saw the quick flash of a torch a long way ahead.

I turned off, away from where I thought the castle lay, pulling Delia after me. Bushes rustled as we stumbled through them, but there was water burbling ahead to cover our sound. The stream had cut a deep path between its banks and we had to climb down. We could have tried to jump across, but at the risk of a great splashing if we jumped short. We waded through and climbed out with wet feet. We were climbing a slope and soon we came to the small conifers. To push through would have fetched our pursuers to the noise; but they had been planted on ridge-and-furrow. We got down and crawled. It took time, but at least we were still moving and in comparative silence. I thought that we were heading back roughly along the route I had followed as a beater and that we would come out on an estate road not far from Mr Taylor's house.

We came out of the conifers at the crest of the slope

just as the moon, still rising, cleared the fringe of cloud and emerged finally into open sky.

My sense of direction had betrayed me. The moon was not where I had expected it to be and the long clearing looked totally unfamiliar. Or perhaps I had passed that way before but could not recognise it by moonlight. I was trying to orient myself from a faint memory of the estate map when we heard a stick break not far away. We froze. The sound was not repeated. It might have been made by a deer, but to our nervous imaginations it was the footfall of a man.

We turned away from the sound and headed along the clearing, only to see the flash of a torch ahead of us. We stopped. I repeated my supersonic whistle – at least, I hoped that it was supersonic – and turned to push through scattered gorse-bushes towards the trees from which we had come.

A man came out of the trees. It was the thin man with the hot eyes, although under the moon his eyes were dark sockets in a white face. He was pointing a large revolver at me. Every detail showed clearly in the moonlight. It looked like the Smith and Wesson Distinguished Combat Magnum, a powerful and accurate weapon, and he was holding it as though he knew how to use it. I froze.

He groped towards me, feeling with his feet for level ground free of roots and rabbit holes, never taking his eyes off his point of aim which was somewhere in the vicinity of my navel. He came to a halt when the revolver was only a few inches from the middle pop-stud of Dad's coat. The hammer was cocked and his finger was on the trigger. My stomach tried to crawl up and hide in my rib-cage.

'Drop it,' he said.

I let go of my steel bar.

'Where's the other one?'

I had thought that Delia was still behind me. Moving very slowly in case a sudden movement caused him to clamp on the trigger, I cocked an eye over one shoulder and then the other. I seemed to be alone with him. If Delia had taken off for the hills, I could hardly blame her.

'I don't know,' I said.

The revolver lifted until it was pointed between my eyes. 'It's a waste of a juicy piece of tail,' he said harshly, 'but if we've got to look for her it'll be quicker without you. Tell me now or kiss yourself goodbye.'

'She was here a minute ago,' I said feebly. Why couldn't the moon go in again? And where the hell had Delia gone? Miserable, cowardly, feeble infant!

'If that's the way you want it.'

I was braced to make a futile run for it when Delia – blessed, brave, beautiful Delia – rose out of a gorse-bush behind him and swung the steel bar. She must have taken my words to heart, because she swung it with all her might. I ducked hurriedly to the side, as much as anything to avoid her swing which seemed capable of taking both our heads off. The whack of steel on bone merged with the stunning slam of a .357 magnum cartridge fired just above my head and I felt a slap from the hot gasses on the back of my neck. He folded down at my feet.

'Have I killed him?' Delia asked hopefully.

'With luck,' I said. 'Well done! Come on.' I grabbed up the revolver. My steel bar I left where it was. The revolver alone weighed more than three pounds and any-way Delia was a better hand at head-butting than I would have been. I had spent many hours target-shooting with

Dad and the revolver felt comfortably familiar to my hand.

There was a shout not far away and the sound of somebody crashing through undergrowth.

We ran across the clearing and plunged between thin pine-trees. There was a shot from behind us and I felt a dozen stings, but they were so far apart, ranging from my ankle to my shoulder-blade, that I knew, without having to think about it, that the shotgunner was out of serious range. I made up my mind that he was not going to get any closer and live. Delia seemed to be untouched.

The ground fell away again steeply, and we went down in one great leap and slither, sometimes rebounding from tree to tree but unwilling and unable to slow down until we arrived at the bottom. We ran out onto one of the estate roads but, disoriented and by moonlight, I didn't recognise it. I was totally lost.

A man was skittering down the hill after us, appearing and vanishing in the shadows between the trees. The moonlight flickered back from some sort of firearm. He would reach the bottom before we could be out of shotgun range. I cocked and hefted the revolver. Dad owned a similar model but with the four-inch instead of the six-inch barrel. The balance was slightly different.

If I killed him, the law would not blame me. But something inside me rebelled at taking a human life, even the life of a man who had just taken a shot at me. I took aim just in front of his feet and fired, expecting to hit him about the knee.

The weight and balance absorbed much of the heavy recoil. The revolver failed to kick up and I hit the ground at his feet, throwing up a spray of twigs and pebbles. The result was almost as satisfactory as if I had shot his leg off, because his involuntary jump cost him his balance and he finished the steep descent in a long tumble and roll, finishing ten yards from us. It was quicker to run towards him than away. I reached him before he could recover himself. He sat up slowly. The barrel of a shotgun was underneath him.

The man who had goosed me, twice grabbed me and then slapped me, now stared back at me. Even by moonlight he must have seen my swollen face and the hatred in my one open eye. My compunction faded away. I brought the revolver up and pointed it between his eyes.

This time, he did not smile. He put his hands over his face as though to deflect a bullet. And in the silence, while I was still nerving myself, I heard a small sound as his bowels let go.

That evidence of his fear was so human that my determination lapsed again. If I had not been quivering with nerves and high on adrenalin, I would have broken down and howled with laughter. Instead, I swung the revolver. Through his fingers he saw the blow coming and tried to turn his head. I caught him across the bridge of the nose. Blood sprayed and I heard the cartilage break. He moaned but he was still conscious and a hurt man may still be a danger. I swung the revolver back and caught him on the side of the head.

He rolled over and lay still. If he was not out cold he was remarkably good at 'playing possum'.

My hands and knees were quivering, but I managed to pull the shotgun out from under him. It was a cheap repeater. If the magazine capacity had been reduced to suit the new legislation, there could not be more than two rounds in it, but I did not feel like waiting around to search the recumbent man. I told Delia to drop her bar and handed her the shotgun.

'Two down and two to go,' I added.

'I couldn't shoot this,' she said.

She certainly couldn't have handled the revolver. (What, I wondered, do they teach girls in school these days?) 'You won't have to do anything clever,' I said. 'Just point it and pull the trigger. The gun will do the rest. But whatever you do, keep it pointing away from me.' My mouth had gone dry. I worked up a little saliva and gave another whistle, held it for as long as my breath would allow and, on a blind guess, led us away to the right.

For the moment our remaining pursuers seemed to have lost touch with us, but they must have been homing in on the sound of the shot. I decided to cover some distance and then get off the road and go to ground. Two men would not be enough for a thorough search and Farquharson must know that he was running out of time.

Several minutes later I thought that we had come far enough, but the estate road was running between mature pines and the ground beneath them offered little cover. There was a sound in the air. It took me a few seconds to recognise it as the beat of the motorbike, throttled down for silence. It seemed to come from all around but it was growing louder every moment. Soon I was sure that it was coming from up ahead.

I gave Delia a push. 'Get behind a thick tree and stand still.'

I made for the stoutest trunk I could see, growing close beside the narrow road. As I reached it, my foot tripped on something. I stooped. It was a fallen branch as thick as my arm and when I took hold of it I found that it was about four feet long, a formidable weapon. I laid the revolver carefully at the base of the tree where I could be sure of finding it again and tucked myself up against the trunk.

The motorcycle was coming, too fast for the rough and narrow road, throttled back but in high gear. A blaze of light lit the scene for a few seconds before he put his headlamp off again. He was just about to pass my tree.

I stepped out and swung my heavy weapon.

I nearly missed him. The road was narrow but he was off-centre. The branch was just long enough to catch the end of his handlebar.

The effect was dramatic. The front wheel turned suddenly and the bike lay down and skidded. The rider travelled on. Memory insists that he was still in a seated position like some cartoon character, but that can't be so because he landed on his face ten yards further on, bounced into a somersault with limbs whirling in every direction and curled himself around the base of another tree just as the sliding motorbike caught up with him. The engine coughed twice more and then stalled.

We left him alone. We had enough guns and he was not going to return to the fray for a long, long time.

Three down and only Farquharson remained. Or had he already given up and left for Dunbar?

Ahead was what looked like a thick stand of trees. It might be a good place to go to ground. He would be lucky to find us again by moon- and torchlight and he might not be keen to poke around in the dark if he guessed that we now had guns. We might even be able to ambush him. If he threatened us, I decided that I would have no compunction this time. I had taken enough from Mr Farquharson.

134

All was quiet as we neared the trees. I pulled Delia onto the grass verge, ready to push into the thick cover. And then a voice spoke out of the darkness.

'Stop right there and put the guns down in front of you.' A voice with the habit of command, Nigel Farquharson's voice. 'Do it. I can still use hostages but I can manage very well without.'

Alone, I might have run for it. If he was armed with a pistol or a rifle, I could probably have got away. I looked round, hoping that Delia had done her vanishing act. She was standing beside me, pointing the shotgun vaguely in the direction of the trees.

'Do as he says,' I told her tiredly. I laid the big revolver down. As I did so, I whistled again.

'And stop making that stupid noise,' he said. 'I've been following you by the sound of it.'

Delia was sobbing and I saw that she was sucking her thumb again. As I came down from my high into a swamp of depression my pellet-wounds, my face, my neck, my hands, all began to hurt. I also felt faintly aggrieved. A shooting man in late middle age had no right to good hearing at that high pitch.

He came out of the wood, carrying a side-by-side shotgun. Again my butterfly mind recognised it immediately. It was one of the Army and Navy sidelocks made by the underrated firm of Squires and Hodges.

We stood. My mind, once so full of ideas, had emptied itself.

Footsteps sounded along the estate road. Farquharson raised his voice. 'About bloody time,' he said loftily.

I felt myself slide from depression towards panic. Farquharson, on his own, might have kept us for hostages and driven us to Dunbar. Once there, rather than kill us within sight or sound of his crewman, he might have left us tied up in one of his Land Rovers on the harbour wall. It was a thin hope but at least it was a hope of sorts. But we had left behind us a trail of injured men. If one of those had recovered, we could expect no mercy at all.

A figure came along the road at a smart trot. The face was in shadow but I thought for an uneasy moment that it was the man I had clubbed with the revolver. Then, as he came closer, I recognised Mr Taylor, the keeper. He was carrying a rather nice old Westley Richards hammer-gun.

'What's adae?' he asked his boss. 'I heard shots. Thought we had the poachers again.'

'It's nothing,' Farquharson said. 'Go back to your house.'

At the risk of endangering the keeper's life along with our own, I had to grasp at the precious straw. 'Don't go,' I said desperately. 'Our lives are in danger. Your boss is a criminal.'

Mr Taylor hesitated, visibly doubtful. Farquharson might be his boss but the keeper had known me for years. I wondered how much weight that would carry. He had known me since I was a schoolgirl much given to practical jokes; and, as Ian says, people tend to remember the follies of youth before they notice the wisdom of maturity. The habit of a lifetime was balanced against his judgement.

'I never heard such libellous nonsense,' Farquharson said loudly. 'If you value your job, Taylor, go away and leave us to sort this thing out.'

'Your job's up the spout anyway,' I said. 'If Mr Farquharson doesn't get out of the country tonight, he'll be arrested. If you don't believe me, this is the girl who was kidnapped. Ask her.'

136

There was a silence that lasted for a dozen heartbeats. I counted them. An owl passed silently overhead, intent on its own small drama, but nobody looked up. Only its shadow under the moon flitted across the ground between us. Then Mr Taylor made up his mind. The barrels of the Westley Richards came up. It would have been against his training and every instinct to point them directly at Farquharson, but they were pointing very close to his boss's toes. The keeper moved in front of me.

'I'll bide and hear this out,' he said quietly. 'There's no skaith coming to either of these lasses while I'm around.'

'He acted for Sir Humphrey Peace in a fiddle over the Sempylene shares,' I said.

Farquharson looked around uncertainly, but none of his men was in sight. There were three of us facing him. Mr Taylor was holding a gun and there were two more at our feet. If Farquharson wanted to stake his life, he could fire two shots and then he would have to reload. Delia might have been an unknown quantity but he must have known that I could shoot. It was a difficult decision, but one that he had to make for himself.

'It's a lot of damned nonsense,' he said at last. 'The police may have been poking around but they never found a shadow of a connection between Sir Humphrey and me. I'd never met the man until this young woman introduced us, at her wedding. Do as I tell you, Taylor. Go back to your house and your wife and don't meddle with matters that aren't your business.'

'I can tell them about a connection,' I said.

'Oh, can you indeed?' said Farquharson grimly. 'I should like to hear about that.'

'And so would I,' said a new voice. We all turned.

137

From the trees on the other side of the road Ian emerged, towed by old Sam whose tail was going like a mad thing. 'You'd better put that down,' Ian told Farquharson. 'There are armed officers all around. That's what the delay was,' he added to me. 'I had to assemble a posse. As soon as we moved off, Sam led us straight to you. I take it that you were whistling?'

'Like a kettle,' I said. I would have thrown myself at him except that he was obviously being a policeman for the moment rather than a husband. 'Where's Dad's gun?' I asked.

'It's in a safe place. I'm not authorised to go armed.' Ian was speaking to me but his eyes were on Delia.

'And the jeep?'

'Also safe. Hello Delia. I'm relieved to see you. Are you all right?'

When I had asked the same question she had seemed uncertain as to the answer, but now she nodded energetically.

I thought that Ian might have been bluffing, but torches were appearing among the trees and policemen, some uniformed and others in plain clothes, came out on to the road. About half of them were indeed armed. Farquharson sighed and unloaded his gun. 'Look after it,' he said, handing it to the nearest officer. 'I'm holding you responsible.'

Sam was trying to knock me over so that he could lick me. I knelt down and put my arms around him. That drew Ian's attention to my face. 'What happened to you?' he asked grimly. 'Did this prisoner hit you?'

'Another man hit me,' I said. 'The one with the freshly broken nose. He also put some shotgun pellets into me. No, I'm not bleeding to death,' I said, as Ian made a sudden movement towards me. 'They just feel like bruises for the moment. He's somewhere in the woods, probably still unconscious. And there are two others. One of them may still be armed. We knocked them out,' I added carelessly.

'Did you by God!' Ian said. 'Could one of you lead us to them?'

'I could do that,' Delia said eagerly. In all the excitement she seemed to have forgotten about being cold, but one of the policemen found her a spare anorak.

Ian detailed two men to take charge of Mr Farquharson and others to go with Delia. The self-important Sergeant Ferless arrived, panting. 'Whistle up the van, and the doctor if he's standing by,' Ian told him. 'Now,' he said to me, 'tell me the connection between Sir Humphrey Peace and this . . . gentleman.'

'I don't have to stand around here and listen to this nonsense,' Nigel Farquharson said. 'I'm going back to the castle. I'll wait for you there, to come and apologise.'

'He has a boat at Dunbar,' I told Ian. Mr Farquharson gave me a look which, as far as I could tell in the poor light, was reproachful.

'You'll stay where you are,' Ian said shortly. 'Now, Deborah. What's the connection?'

But I was not going to go on before punishing him a little bit. 'You knew all along that Mr Farquharson had been the biggest purchaser of Sempylene shares during the takeover,' I said.

He shrugged. 'If we could have found any connection between them, even one single acquaintance in common other than you and your family, there would have been an arrest long ago. But your father was adamant that they met for the first time at our wedding.'

'That was a bluff,' I said. 'To bolster it up, Mr Farquharson said something which was the biggest insult one shooting man can hand out to another and Sir Humphrey only looked amused. I thought it was odd at the time.'

Ian nodded slowly. 'A hundred others bought shares. There was a rumour in one of the tabloids that the firm was going to survive – planted, I'd guess, to give them an out if questions were ever raised. But that wasn't my part of the case and I didn't even know that Farquharson lived at Boyes Castle until you mentioned it.' Ian paused and blew out a deep breath. 'I nearly told you to turn around and drive home. It was only on your assurance that Mr Taylor was trustworthy that I agreed to approach him.'

'And I was right,' I pointed out.

'So you were. Now, what was the connection?'

Short of making him say 'please', I had pushed it as far as it would go. 'You were asking the wrong people the wrong questions. Sir Humphrey and Mr Farquharson are members of the same rather exclusive club,' I said. 'I've no proof that they ever met, but the club holds an annual dinner. They probably met there and did the rest of their business by phone. Somebody can tell you whether they sat at the same table.'

'What club?'

'The Woodcock Club. It's only open to people who've shot a right-and-left at woodcock in front of witnesses – which is very much more difficult than you'd think. They come at you low and fast and suddenly. I nearly achieved it once but I was over-excited and I missed the second one.'

140

'I never heard such nonsense,' Farquharson said. Hemmed in between the two policemen, he looked smaller. I wondered how I had ever come to feel in awe of him.

'But you're wearing the club tie,' I said. 'I noticed it as soon as you came into the garage. Sir Humphrey was wearing the same tie when he came out on the search-party.'

'Not true,' Farquharson said in a low voice, almost a whisper. 'One of my guests left this tie in the house and I liked it. That's all there is to it.'

'It'll be in the club's records,' I said.

Mr Taylor had been standing by, so still and silent that we had forgotten him. 'No,' he said suddenly. 'No. I was one of the laird's two witnesses when he joined the club.' He looked at his employer while choosing his next words. He was torn by conflicting emotions but professional respect came out on top. 'Even if your second shot was gey near the beating line, Mr Farquharson, that was a damned fine right-and-left.'

For a moment, I thought that the laird of Boyes Castle was going to persist in his denials. Perhaps pride intervened. 'Yes,' he said slowly. 'It was, wasn't it?' He turned away between the two officers.

Eight

Despite the presence of shotgun pellets under the skin he loved to touch, Ian was in no rush to pack me off to hospital but at least he had sent for the doctor. The 'van', when it arrived, groping uncertainly around the estate roads, turned out to be a sort of minibus, probably more often used for transporting prisoners to and from court, and I was invited inside.

At that point, we arrived at a double impasse. I had no intention of undressing, even for a doctor, in an illuminated van where any policeman lurking in the darkness outside could enjoy the show. The doctor, however, quite understood. He was one of those hearty doctors who should never be allowed to practise medicine. He remarked that none of the three pellets visible in my legs was serious and that the others, having passed through Dad's waxproof, could certainly wait. He confirmed that if I had had any concussion it had already passed off and – heartlessly, I thought – he said that the damage to the coat was probably more serious than the damage to my skin. He confirmed that neither Delia nor I would be endangered by a slight delay while brief statements were taken in the back of the van.

It was then that I was invited to sit down to make my

statement and I discovered for the first time that one of the pellets was lodged just where it would be pressed between the hard seat and the lowest corner of my pelvic girdle. I made my statement from a kneeling position.

The flashing light of an ambulance was visible further along the estate road, but I could not see whether the stretchers being placed aboard were covered. Ian brought me up to date. To my secret relief, none of Nigel Farquharson's three hirelings was dead when found, although Delia's victim was still unconscious and the motor-cyclist had enough broken bones to qualify for inclusion in the *Guinness Book of Records*.

Delia herself, when she was brought back from the successful search for injured toughs, was in control of herself. Indeed, she was a bit carried away with her own contribution to our escape. Her manner to me had returned to its old adulation, but there was a tendency for my actions or decisions to be attributed to 'us' while our joint activities seemed to be her own.

After that, we were left alone in the back of the van for a few minutes until Ian called me outside.

'I want you to break it to Delia about her father,' he said.

'You do it,' I told him.

He flinched visibly. The bravest men often balk at breaking bad news to women. 'The news isn't as bad as it might have been,' he said. 'I've just had word. He's going to live. In fact, he's awake and talking.'

That put rather a different complexion on it. 'But she thinks that her father's still bouncing with health and you want me to break it to her that he's badly injured,' I said.

'It would come better from a woman. Besides, she trusts you.'

I told him that he was a louse, climbed back into the van and asked Delia to brace herself for bad news. She took it better than I could have expected. After the first impact, she wiped her eyes and blew her nose and then nothing would do but that she be taken to see him immediately.

Time seemed to have slipped away unnoticed and I wished that I could do the same. By now, midnight was near. In the meantime a more senior officer, whom I had not met before and never saw again, had arrived to take over and to steal such credit as remained unclaimed. Ian could now be spared and, when I pointed out that a visit from Delia would soothe the minds and might liberate the tongues of both father and daughter, he was delegated to take her in to Edinburgh. Because I was overdue for attention in one hospital or another, I was nominated to go along and play chaperone and comforter. I would rather have obtained treatment locally and gone home to bed, but nobody was paying much attention to my wishes.

Delia and I, and a rather anxious Sam who had missed his dinner, were put in the back of a police car. Ian got in beside the driver and we were driven, at great speed and with lights and klaxon going, to Edinburgh. I travelled in a twisted position, taking my weight on one hip and risking the addition of a slipped disc to my other woes.

Sam was left in the car. The driver promised to walk him. I was the first to be dropped off, at Accident and Emergency. By then, spots of dried blood had glued my clothes to the puncture wounds which were definitely tender. Once those adhesions had been soaked away, the removal of a dozen shotgun pellets from not too

144

deep under my skin was unpleasant but comparatively bearable. Only time, I was told, would heal my bruised face. The punctures, plus a score of other small wounds, were dressed with adhesive plasters.

I was more distressed by sheer hunger. The thought of Sam's dinner had reminded me that I had not eaten since Mrs Taylor's soup on what was now the previous day. My heartfelt grumbles on that score persuaded a friendly nurse to go and forage in the kitchens and she brought me a hot meat pie, a slab of cake and a whole flask of coffee.

When at last I was fed, lead-free, sterilised, Elastoplasted and dressed again in clothes that Oxfam would have rejected, the same nurse led me through miles of mostly silent corridors and pointed me in the direction of the Intensive Care unit where Bernard Thrower still lay.

A big hospital never quite sleeps. Like a cat at rest, the body may seem relaxed but there is always a pulse of activity and a readiness to respond to any sudden emergency. Soft footsteps sound amid dim lighting and here and there will be sudden splashes of bright lights and the sound of voices. I followed voices to a side-ward and stopped in the doorway.

A bandaged figure was lying prone in the bed, attached by tubes and wires to all the paraphernalia made familiar by hospital epics on televison. Somebody was speaking huskily above the reassuring bleep of some kind of monitor and I recognised the voice of Bernard Thrower. Delia was sitting beside the bed, holding tight to his hand. Ian was standing at the foot of the bed and a constable squatting in a hard chair was trying to take shorthand on his knee.

The scene, evoking pain and damaged bodies, made me shiver. I was about to turn away when Ian said, 'Go on. When did you first realise that the rules were being broken?'

This was interesting. I waited around the corner where I could hear without seeing or being seen. A soft-footed passer-by in a white coat with a lapel badge looked at me curiously but decided not to bother.

'The purchases of shares came back to me for registration,' Thrower said. His voice was weak but firm. 'Several names cropped up about which I had my doubts. Not the directors themselves, but people I guessed to be connected with them.'

'Can you give me any examples?' Ian asked.

Bernard Thrower's laugh turned into a grunt of pain. 'With no difficulty,' he said. 'For instance, the sales director's a tough old boot named Mrs Jenson. I happened to know, because I had noticed it when registering her with BUPA, that her maiden name was McAllister; and no less than three McAllisters turned up among the purchasers. I spoke to Sir Humphrey, but he laughed it off. He said that you couldn't expect somebody with that sort of information not to give a hint to an aunt or a cousin.

'I wasn't satisfied. It still smacked of insider trading to me, but he was the chairman.'

'So you did nothing about it?'

'Before—' Thrower choked on the word. 'Thirsty,' he said in a whisper. There were sounds as somebody, probably Delia, gave him a drink. When he spoke again, his voice was stronger. 'Thank you, my dear. Before I could make up my mind what if anything to do about it, something else happened. Sir Humphrey and I had been to a meeting in Edinburgh about the takeover and we decided to have lunch at the North British Hotel. I went

146

to the toilet and as I came back into the room I saw Mr Farquharson stop and speak to Sir Humphrey.'

I realised with a jump that another eavesdropper was standing beside me. Sir Peter Hay had arrived. He winked at me and put his finger to his lips.

'You knew Nigel Farquharson?' Ian asked.

'By sight. My previous employer had done business with him, so when his name cropped up as a major purchaser of shares it caught my attention. I knew that his business had been badly hit by the slump in shipping and foreign competition, flags of convenience and so on; so he was hardly likely to have large sums of "risk money" available.'

'When he spoke to Sir Humphrey,' Ian said, 'did they seem to know each other?'

'There was no doubt in my mind at all. Mr Farquharson first looked around to be sure that nobody was watching and then patted Sir Humphrey on the shoulder. He was smiling.' I heard a sigh. 'It shook me up. Sir Humphrey had been very good to me. He gave me my job and nursed me through the early stages when I thought that I'd taken on more than I could handle. I looked up to him. But it was too much of a coincidence that the biggest purchaser of shares should turn out to be his friend. I . . . I couldn't face him after that. I'd already made up my mind to leave home and go to Elaine Anderton. Do you mind very much?'

The question did not make sense until I realised that he was speaking to Delia, who said, 'No,' in a small but firm voice.

'That's good. So I just walked out of the hotel and never even went back to the office. I didn't think they'd seen me, but they must have done. I suppose that that put the wind up them.'

'Probably not as much as did your sudden disappearance,' Ian said. 'The two taken together caused a real fluttering in the dovecot. Somebody weeded out the office files, making it very difficult for us to prove exactly when some directors came by the knowledge that they used so improperly and you were the one uninvolved person who could make sense of it for us. In the office, you might have been controlled, pressured by loyalties or the promise of promotion. On the loose, you were a threat.'

'I never thought of it that way,' Mr Thrower said. 'It didn't occur to me to look at my position from their point of view. If I had, I might have realised that I was putting Delia at risk. I'm sorry, Baby.'

If Delia said anything, I missed hearing it because Ian spoke again. 'Can you help us? And will you?'

'Of course. After the way Delia was treated, I wish I could do more. I kept a working diary of the whole transaction. I suppose somebody shredded the hard copy, but the text will still be stored in the desktop computer in my room. I don't expect that anybody thought to wipe it. You'll need the security code, of course.'

'And you can give it to me?'

'Whenever you're ready.'

'You carry it in your head?'

'Where else would it be safe?'

Sir Peter touched my arm and led me away, round a turn of the corridor.

'That tidies it up very nicely,' he said with satisfaction. 'Now that the facts are in the open they'll get the evidence. Well done, young lady! Now I can go on with finalising the takeover and then hand over and get back to sanity and the quiet life.'

'You've enjoyed it,' I said.

He slowed to a halt. 'It's fun to have power for a while, but it's very tiring. God must get fed up, sometimes. By the way, congratulations on your escape and the rescue of Delia. I understand that you laid about you to such effect that an ambulanceful of the ungodly were removed from the grounds of Boyes Castle.'

I nearly asked him how he came to know about it so quickly, but there would have been no point. Sir Peter seems to be on intimate terms with absolutely everybody and he always knows everything long before anybody else. 'Delia sloshed one of them,' I said. 'Two were mine and Ian arrested Mr Farquharson before I could lay a finger on him.'

'A pity,' said Sir Peter. 'He deserved to have you let loose on him. But never mind. The law will descend on him from an even greater height. And on Humphrey Peace. I never could abide that man. Too full of himself to hold anything else.' He beamed at me.

'If it's all over,' I said, 'perhaps I can go home for a meal, sleep and try to get the business back on the road.'

He looked at me again with his shaggy eyebrows raised. 'It's not quite over,' he said. 'The solution to a crime never solves the human consequences. As soon as we got the news, I brought Elaine Anderton through.'

'You did?'

'Of course. She's been staying with m'ladyship and me, the last few days. That husband of yours suggested it. Clever young chap! It seemed the best answer. When we heard that her – um – boyfriend was conscious, she was busting to come through and be a ministering angel or something.'

'That seems to have all the makings of a happy ending.'

His smile faded. 'Not quite. Over the phone, I gathered that the news is not all up to its face value. Also, the official Mrs Thrower is around here somewhere, looking for a doctor to spill the beans. If and when those two meet the fur will fly, the cat will be among the pigeons and, to introduce yet another metaphor, we may see a mushroom cloud.'

'I see,' I said unhappily. And I did. If it came to a hair-pulling, face-scratching free-for-all – and restrained women like Mrs Thrower are often the first to lose all control – Sir Peter would be too gentlemanly to wrench them apart. As Ian says, it takes two to make a quarrel and two to break up a fight. I was not looking forward to the next few minutes. My aches and pains were catching up with me and I now knew what it would be like to feel very, very old. 'Can't we keep them apart?' I suggested.

'We could try.'

'You could take Elaine away again.'

'She wouldn't go,' he said simply.

We found Miss Anderton sitting nervously in an alcove that passed for a waiting-room. She jumped to her feet. 'Can I see him now?' she asked.

Sir Peter patted her shoulder in his most fatherly manner. She seemed to take some comfort from the contact. 'Soon,' he said. 'The police are taking his statement. And if you see a doctor first, you'll have a better idea of what to say. And, of course, what not to say, which is usually much more important.'

'I suppose so.'

Mrs Thrower appeared a few seconds later, but we were spared the worst effects of the 'critical mass'. Mrs Thrower called Elaine Anderton a promiscuous, predatory, knickerless slut and Miss Anderton called the older woman a frigid, heartless, uncaring old bitch in chainmail drawers but, perhaps because Sir Peter and I kept between them, there was no attempt at violence. Their voices rose. Remembering that it was night-time in a hospital I tried to hush them but I was ignored. The two ladies were now speaking simultaneously, each trying to shout the other down and drawing on a wealth of imaginative vituperation that I would have supposed to have been beyond them. Sir Peter seemed fascinated and I had the impression that he was enjoying the episode. I stored away as much of the dialogue as I could memorise, for repeating to Ian.

The debate was cut short by the arrival of a doctor who cleared his throat loudly. It took some seconds for the abuse to cease as neither was prepared to suppress some choice epithet nor to fall silent and leave the initiative to the other. Their voices tailed away at last.

'I understood that Mr Thrower's relatives were here and wanted to be informed about his condition,' the doctor said severely. 'Perhaps I was misinformed.'

'You were not,' said Mrs Thrower. 'I am his wife.'

'His estranged wife,' said Elaine Anderton firmly. 'I'm his fiancée.'

Explosion once again seemed imminent but the doctor, although he looked very young, seemed to have experienced such collisions in the past. 'Before you come to any decisions about Mr Thrower's future,' he said, 'perhaps you'd better hear what I have to say.'

Mrs Thrower, who had been muttering darkly, broke off. 'What do you mean?' she asked.

'Your husband's life is out of danger, but at that point the good news stops.'

The two froze. I think that we all did. Elaine Anderton asked the doctor what he meant.

The doctor looked down at his clipboard. He took a deep breath and then plunged ahead. 'The spinal damage is severe. It seems unlikely that Mr Thrower will ever walk again. Of course, there is always hope. You were told that his prospect of survival was negligible, yet he survived. But miracles, like lightning, seldom strike twice in the same place. You can take it as a virtual certainty that he'll be in hospital for some months and then tied to his bed or a wheelchair for the rest of his life.' There was a long pause. 'I'm sorry,' he said. He looked up at the ceiling, making it clear that his words were addressed to neither woman in particular. 'When you've come to terms with the basic facts, the consultant would like to see you; and before Mr Thrower eventually leaves hospital, the physiotherapists will be able to give you a great deal of useful advice.' He wheeled about and hurried away. Relief at having delivered his news and made his escape was written all over his back.

Mrs Thrower pursed her thin lips. She was the first to break the silence. 'I know my duty,' she said.

'Oh, poor Bernard!' Elaine Anderton burst out. 'How can you talk of duty?'

'At least I can see where duty lies. Some people have a blind spot when duty conflicts with their personal lusts. He won't have anything to interest you now that his sex-life is over. I think you'll find that his days of adultery are done. But I shall forgive him.'

Elaine Anderton opened her mouth, no doubt to say something cataclysmic, but Sir Peter turned his head towards her. I could not see what kind of look he directed at her, but it stopped her in mid-syllable.

'I'm sure that you'll manage very well,' Sir Peter told Mrs Thrower. 'You're a fine, strong woman, well able to lift an invalid in and out of his bed or the bath. Of course, your husband won't be capable of earning, but there are grants available from the local authorities.'

A movement in the shadows of the corridor caught my eye. Delia, banished from her father's side, was waiting to join us.

'I know my duty,' Mrs Thrower said again but with rather less certainty. I decided that she had been picturing a return to her old lifestyle, with occasional pauses to mop her husband's brow and give orders to the nurse. A life of dedication, on handouts from what remains of the Welfare State, did not have the same appeal.

Elaine Anderton had been standing with her mouth open. She closed it suddenly. 'Do you really think that he'd want you to care for him as a duty?' she asked. Her voice began to rise and she fumbled for words, but her sincerity was manifest. 'You're cold. You'd feel martyred and you'd let him know it. He'd need love and you'd expect gratitude. Well, that seems to me to be a poor bargain from his viewpoint. I love him,' she said more gently, 'and I'll look after him for as long as he needs me, as an act of love. There won't be any money, but we'll manage somehow.'

Mrs Thrower tossed her head. She made a small sound indicative of indignation and contempt, but I could detect signs of relief. She hesitated. She might not want to commit herself to a lifetime of nursing a crippled husband, but

153

her self-image would not let her jump too eagerly into this escape route. 'If that's how you feel about it—' she began.

'It's exactly how I feel about it,' said Elaine.

It was nothing to do with me, but I felt I had to stick my oar in. 'What about Delia?' I asked.

'Delia will always have a home with me,' said Mrs Thrower.

'You make it sound like another duty,' said Elaine. 'I think that Delia should choose for herself.'

Delia moved out of the shadows of the corridor where she had been standing, unseen by the others. She walked sedately and there was a new maturity about her. During our escape through the grounds of Boyes Castle, she had managed to take ruthless action on her own initiative. This, and exposure to some of the harsher realities of life, had helped her to grow up in a hurry. 'Dad already told me,' she said. 'I want to be where he is. I'm quite strong. Perhaps I can help. He doesn't want to be a burden if he's not wanted, but I know that he'd rather be with Elaine. He said so.' The effect of her words was spoiled by a huge yawn at the end. It was long past her bedtime. And mine.

'So be it,' said Mrs Thrower. 'I shall go to my sister in Oban. I'll leave your clothes and things with Mrs Calder.' She looked once at each of us and she turned away. Delia watched her go. Then she moved towards her father's lover and in a sudden rush of emotion they put their arms around each other. I looked away from a scene that seemed too personal to be watched.

'Life may not be quite as difficult as you think,' Sir Peter said gently. He offered them a large white handkerchief to share between them. 'Bernard wrote to the firm, offering his resignation, but it was never accepted. It couldn't be, without a return address. I think we can stretch a point and assume that the then chairman was responsible for his absence from duty. So his BUPA membership stands and he'll have a pension coming.'

When I got the old devil alone, I told him. 'You were careful not to say anything about the money while Mrs Thrower was with us.'

He had offered to run me back to where the jeep was waiting for me. We were walking across the empty hospital car park, looking for the police car so that I could collect Sam. Sir Peter's face was in darkness, but when the light of one of the few lamps caught the highlights I thought that he was smiling to himself.

'Of course I was,' he said. 'If I'd mentioned it any sooner, the wife might have put up more of a fight; and I wouldn't wish that on the poor devil. That Miss Anderton's a soft-hearted creature, for all that she's got some backbone. Her love will thrive on his dependence. He'll be much better off with her.'

'So will Delia,' I said.

Sam, when we found him, had been sharing bag after bag of potato crisps with the driver and was in no hurry to get out of the warm police car. I walked away a few yards and gave vent to my special whistle, which brought him out to me with a rush and probably woke up all the younger patients in the hospital. Sir Peter never blinked.